Sufani Weisman-Garza

1377 RIKOPPE L ANE

Sufani Weisman-Garza

About the Author

Sufani has written over a dozen books throughout her life, has been published in many print and digital magazines for health, wellness, and spirituality, and has published poetry. She was an advice columnist for a healing magazine and currently writes the health and wellness section for a monthly color print magazine In Washington State. She is a sole proprietor running a successful international online academy, (www.placeofblissacademy.com) and a private practice offering alternative healing and therapy. She enjoys her clairvoyant gift and uses her real-life experiences to fuel the pages of her fiction thrillers and non-fiction. She lives with her husband, rescue Chihuahua, Minuet her familiar and has three grown children.

1377 Rikoppe Lane

To all my spiritual brothers and sisters who know ghosts are real, this is for you!

I would like to thank my dear husband for putting up with all the ghosts I bring into the house and never complaining about it.

Sufani Weisman-Garza

Table of Contents

Sufani Weisman-Garza

Sufani Weisman-Garza

Sufani Weisman-Garza

One

It was October, almost Halloween time and the weather was beginning to get chilly. The room was ice cold in the morning elements, all windows open in the house as though she were setting something free. She stared off into the void of her living room, her strawberry-colored hair stringy and clinging to her face with bed head in the back as she sat on the edge of her couch clutching a large, meaningless check. Gaylord Carter, *Kings Row*, played in the background – his crazy organ music skipped, then continued, and then skipped again in succession creating an eerie setting of a time gone by. She, having no more tears to cry, abandoned by her husband who had hanged himself in their walk-in closet, was now the ragged mess of a soulless person, with no emotion, poor hygiene, and reduced to a zombie state. A week had passed and the crowds of family and friends who uncomfortably visited her were beginning to subside. A murder of crows took up residence outside her home, her new and annoyingly loud paparazzi. She was grateful for family and friends although she just wanted to disappear. The sincere comments of the loving and awkward had become unbearable. What does someone say to you when their husband would rather be dead than rough it out with you?

"Sorry your man off'd himself?"

"Better luck with your next pick."

There was nothing comfortable to say but "I'm sorry for your loss", which was so inadequate when losing the love of your life. But what else was one to say?

Thoughts raced through her mind, yet she was still disbelieving that this was her new life. She looked down at the check again, reading the rather large amount of money she had received. The large number with zeroes following it was the proof of her husband's knack for financial planning, and the sobering echo of his premeditation. He knew ahead of time he was going to do what he did. He knew he was going to leave her alone in life and did it anyway. That was the most painful of all realizations. He could live without her. He was a kind, tall, African American man in the financial business and knew how to tuck money away, and apparently financially plan his own demise, leaving her with enough money to start a new life. She didn't have to work for some time if that's what she chose.

She spoke with his heartbroken family and would send his cremains back to Benin, his hometown, to be buried after a religious ceremony in their family plot, and this she did after his memorial in the States. Sending him home seemed the right thing to do. She promised to come visit them in the future and visit Clay's final resting place. Right now, she could not imagine how she would ever be able to make that journey, or rather, face it! It was too painful.

She had just turned forty, and was determined to be

sexy as she aged, but in a natural way. Her name was Johannah, she was a subtle but strong person and always managed to stay on the happier side of things. Misery was for novices. She didn't gossip, avoided those who did, and read novels and self-improvement books to enlighten her soul. She was smart and worked in the marketing industry for a local magazine and although it was not her ultimate passion, she was good at it, and it made her a living. She liked the people she met most of all and to her that was what life was about – the people.

Staring at the sand-colored walls, the black furniture pieces, the white floor rugs and all the signs of her husband's style that had always felt a bit too contemporary for her, she suddenly felt like she was in an institution; the edges too square and too sanitary, the African masks now abruptly menacing. She had always liked coming home because he would be there. But now that he wasn't, there was no warmth to her home. The joy he had once imparted was now trumped by his death and the ever-present reminder of his means of exiting the world, and it wasn't pleasant. It just felt cold, and like a place in which she was no longer comfortable. The rage, sadness, discomfort and need to run away from the scene of the crime were building every day. She had to get out of that house and quick. She picked up the phone and called information.

"Dillon Realty, please," she told the operator as they

processed her connection. She would just have Marshall put the condo on the market – fast. She had his number somewhere but had no energy to look for it. He had sold them their house and she wanted to get out of it as fast as possible. "Marshall? Yes, hi, this is Johannah Williams." She paused as he said his condolences. "Thank you. I want to put the house on the market immediately."

There was another pause.

"How fast? Like a bat out of hell. I can't get out of here quick enough!"

Marshal went over his familiar jargon with her briefly and she hung up the phone. The thought of leaving gave her a sense of reprieve drawing near. The only relief she had felt at all since Clay's suicide. She was abandoning ship.

Two

In the car, twisting and turning up a gently winding road, she felt the first sense of peace she could remember feeling in a while. Months had passed since she called Marshall at Dillon Realty. Although not quite the zombie she had been, she had lost some weight unnecessarily that she would have to regain, and had significantly better hygiene, once again restoring her natural good looks. With the car window cracked, she breathed in the fresh harbor air. She thought about the move and starting over. The new house had a fireplace which she planned on bundling up in front of, with the fire going and a bag of sour cream potato chips to start the marathon eating into normal weight range. That always brought her comfort when she was low.

Clay's financial planning allowed her to buy the Victorian house and have enough money for a few years to live modestly on. God knew, the life insurance wasn't going to pay out. She was still heartbroken over Clay's decision to leave this world so soon when they should still have had so much time together, but having no other recourse, she had decided to just move on, and this home and area would have a sort of healing effect on her. Being by the water always did that for her, even as a child. Growing up in Huntington Beach, California and living there all her adult life meant always being ten minutes away from the water. But needing a new start, she opted to leave

13

the state and start over somewhere totally different. No more unannounced visitors: sad faces of uncomfortable awkwardness, and a chance to move on with her life and be happy again. That was all she wanted; to just be happy again. She felt nothing of the sort at the moment, but she felt that, over time, her verve for life may be restored. She hoped. She waited daily for the dull ache of pain and loneliness to subside. Clay's face, as he hung there as she found him, seemed burned into her brain and she had forced herself to see him in her most favorite picture of him; the other was just too painful to remember. She teared up daily and sometimes in the silence of their home together, she sobbed uncontrollably like a child. Once she had removed all her belongings from their room, the door to their bedroom and the closet of his anguished death remained permanently closed. She could never go back in there. She fought daily to remove the last vision of him hanging there lifeless, from his self-inflicted passing. No matter how hard she tried, every time she closed her eyes, she saw him hanging from his tie, knees bent just barely off the floor, hanging from the lower level closet pole, eyes closed as if in shame, and no spirit left in his body. She fought moment by moment to keep that vision out of her head. It had gotten a little easier every day to remember him as he was when they were happy, when he was happy.

Their home sold rather quickly and now she was approaching the new house she had purchased in Gig

Harbor, Washington, a location she picked at random from a YouTube clip she saw as she was searching for lake front cities to possibly move to. Most of the furniture had arrived by container, already waiting for her and the rest she piled into the car with her, the delicate items. The grey sky allowed little beams of sunlight through and leaves crunched under her tires as she approached the old home, passing many other friendly people in large homes, nicely spaced out, unlike where she came from. People waved as though they knew she was coming, while not giving any signs of running over to her immediately to greet her. Already she felt this town was different and perhaps people still maintained the lost art called manners that she grew up with. They seemed friendly and acknowledged her with eye contact and a wave, something that seemed to become more and more retro as the old generations grew up, and the tech generation took over. Life was, however, a pendulum, swinging far to one side only to return back eventually. It was the way of nature. For whatever one generation creates, the next forgets. She always believed in balance and trusted that nature would always even the score, so she didn't worry about it. She just placed herself with people and places that suited her energy to find that balance, and Gig Harbor was that place. At least, she hoped it was, from the pictures and the YouTube ad.

The house was an old Victorian, over a hundred years old, but had been kept up nicely. Perhaps it was in

15

her DNA to feel comfortable and at home in a Victorian home; although she had never lived in one, she was raised by one, her mother, who still had remnants of old Victorian mannerisms; elbows off the table while eating, napkin in lap, shoulders back, only discuss sex when absolutely necessary, and show the proper shame for indecent thoughts, be clean, dust your home and run a finger over the tops of the doors to check for dirt. Yes, she had Victorian blood, and it was like the house and she knew one another instantly. Many of the side windows and the back ones overlooked the water and yet it was also close enough to neighbors and a few minutes from town. She loved the feeling of being tucked away from everyone where she could properly grieve and wallow when she felt like it. Although that wasn't really her style normally, she gave herself the kind allowance of taking the time she needed to get over the feelings she had, allowing herself permission to be negative if she felt like it in those moments she felt betrayed or like a victim. In her old home, around family and friends, she had to appear the perfect version of herself, so as to not alarm them, and in her current state of grief, she was certainly not living up to that mold. However, she wondered why she needed to care for their image of how she was doing when she was the one suffering. She just had to get away, so she could mourn how she wanted, when she wanted, without worrying about how others would respond to her grief. It was too

16

much pressure. She had planned on also taking up counselling to give her someone to talk to about it, just to speed up the process of healing and move on. She pulled into her driveway and instantly recognized the black witch's cap, an old Victorian architectural feature above the large second story bedroom with a wide gazing bay window. She also noticed the less attractive two containers of almost all brand-new furniture; rugs and lighting save for a few items she had decided to keep for sentimental reasons. She had a huge estate sale before she left and got rid of almost everything, so that she could begin again. The decor she and Clay had shared was never her style anyway, but she held on to a few items that preserved his memory. She was more of a shabby chic girl anyhow, eclectic by nature, but she did save Clay's favorite lounging chair and soft blanket that he always had on it. Her personal style allowed her to not commit to any one particular look and she liked that. She smiled at the new house, at the bald large trees hanging over the house like a cloud in the January light. It was midafternoon and it would be getting dark in a few hours so she had to get situated a bit. There was no time to diddle daddle. Looking at the front windows above and then an all-around glance, she saw the house, and strangely it felt as though it looked back at her. Her eyebrows creased at the funny feeling she felt for a moment and then she laughed to herself as she grabbed a few bags from the front seat to go into the house at once.

She loved the front of the house with its wraparound porch and invitation to take a load off. She planned on buying some nice lounges for the front and some tables and comforts. It would be nice to sit out there and just, well, sit! No one did that anymore, but she planned on bringing that experience back. Maybe she could meet others and invite them to sit with her? In time – one step in front of the other. She went to the front door and took out her old-fashioned key, a skeleton key. This home was so old, and no one had chosen to change the key lock system of the front door, something she really loved. She intended to go to the historic society to get more information on the home. She felt it should have become an official historical landmark a long time ago, from the information she had received from the realtor. It was built in 1890 and had been preserved. Funnily enough, this would be the first time she stepped foot in the old house. She bought it sight unseen with her realtor's assurance it was a sound investment. She needed to get out of her state and away from all the sadness. She trusted the photos, and the research of the area stated it was a leisurely crowd in Gig Harbor. *Smithsonian Magazine* said it was one of the 'top five towns for culture, heritage and charm'. Looking around, she believed it. She would have to drive into town and really see how people lived, but from what she had seen so far, it was just what she needed.

Sticking the key in the lock and turning it, the door

Sufani Weisman-Garza

did not budge. She let out a deep sigh. "Really? Ugh!" Her shoulders sank and she rolled her eyes to no one. She tried it again and it did not move. Looking around to the side of the porch she decided to make her way to the back door and try coming in that way. The house was captivating and there was room for parking in the back, and a second house she hadn't been told about – all overlooking the water. She thought how the back houses used to be called maids' quarters. Of course, she wouldn't be calling it that, but was happy to see it there just the same. Going up the narrow stairs to the back door she almost got winded. There were twenty-two half size steps to be exact: an excessive amount in her opinion, but apparently necessary.

"Whew! I need to exercise," she said stepping foot on the landing and taking a deep breath. The back door and all other locks had been updated with current style keys but for some reason the front door had not. She put her more modern key in the door and held her breath. It turned. "Oh, thank God," she let out in relief. "I couldn't take it if you didn't open," she said to the door. Talking to her houses had always been a habit of hers. She had talked to every place she'd lived, believing that the energy of a house responds to its occupants.

She opened the door and walked in. Its breath was stagnant and she was greeted by a small entryway followed by a long hallway that seemed to stretch out longer as she looked down it, peering all the way to the front door. On either side of her were two rooms directly to the left and another kitty corner. Perhaps at one time a sitting or sewing room, drawing room or den, but clearly over the years had been used as bedrooms. She went into the left room and it was quaint, but small, empty, with a window looking out into the backyard grounds, small parking area and a distant view of the water. She walked out of that room, passing a full guest bathroom and into the room on the right. This room was larger and also had a master bath, as well. The window looked out of the side of the house grounds, still allowing for a slight view of the harbor and maids' quarters. Each room was prepared with a rose-colored thick velvet wallpaper design on the walls that she found soothing. Whether it ran throughout the house, she did not yet know. It seemed silly that she bought a house and up until this very moment she had no idea what the inside looked like. In her past, she would have never done such a thing. But life had become unpredictable and her with it.

She walked out of the room and back into the foyer and saw the kitchen; a large, high-ceilinged room with plenty of countertops and a wooden island in the center. She put her keys down on the island and looked around in awe. "Wow!" was all she could muster. She continued through the bottom floor of the house going into the dining room from the kitchen that opened into the dining, and then living room. The ceilings were at least twelve feet

Sufani Weisman-Garza

high and made her feel small as she walked through the rooms. The walls seemed alive, unlike the feeling one gets in a rental apartment or cookie cutter home. The kitchen was beautifully tiled and dining room was papered in deep gold velvet, regal looking wallpaper. It would take her time to get used to the feel of the place. Across from the living room was the front entrance and on the other side was what once must have been the library, slash, sitting room, which was the custom a long time ago. People who visited did not have full access and view of the entire home, just access from the front door to the sitting room, which acted as a waiting room for their host. In such rooms, they would serve tea and biscuits to their guests, and guests were always a special treat upon a home. Not like today where a surprise guest is either trying to sell you something, or there to murder you. Most responses to unannounced guests are to army crawl away from any visible window, as to not be heard inside, so they go away. Times had changed indeed. The house was a reminder of gentler times, a period when manners and social etiquette mattered and spoke for how you were raised. She enjoyed the reminder of that time frame in her own home. More and more, as she went through the house, she was realizing just what a big change it would be and how much she thought she would enjoy living there. Home was a place she wanted to spend a great deal of time in these days. She could be undisturbed with her thoughts, and work out her feelings, free from the discerning eye of the public, family, and friends. It had such a strong presence it was like living with a friend. It had been born long before her.

Every window was heavily draped in mahogany and gold velvet tapestries, with a delicate French sheer drape in the center allowing in light and a view. She could get lost in the feeling of the house. She was used to nice things, but this felt so different. It felt like she was home for some reason and the rooms seem to wrap their energy around her, making her feel safe; something she had not felt since Clay's death. From the library, she went to the front door which was an old door with the top half being a window and she saw her large front yard and car parked in the driveway just past her steep view of the front porch stairs. There were seven full size steps to the house, but they were not as steep as the back porch. The house had so many unique features. Nothing was the same, everything had personality.

She opened the door, which surprisingly was not locked, and she stopped a moment to try to understand why it did not open. She turned the knob which felt a little sticky, like old joints having to move for the first time in a while. "Oh, I see. Your bones are old and stiff. I got it. That's okay, old house. I'm a friend and will take good care of you," she said out loud, looking from ceiling to floor, and all around. She smiled and opened the door and stepped onto the porch, took in a deep breath and wandered back into

22

the house. She needed her keys now to get into the storage unit parked outside. She walked past the stairs that followed the entryway into the hall that led back into the entrance of the kitchen to get her keys. She grabbed them off the kitchen countertop and began walking down the hallway back to the front door and went from a speedy walk to being frozen in her spot. Scratching her head in silence thinking, she had left them on the island. She thought more and turned and tilted her head to really think about it looking back at the kitchen and then the block.

"Hmm, I must have left them where I just got them," she said, laughing to herself. "I need to get it together," she said under her breath and continued out the front door to begin taking things into the house. She left the door open. She was losing light each minute and had to get the basics for a comfortable night's sleep in the house right away, just for the tonight. The rest she'd get in the morning and spend the better part of the day really moving in. After making a few rounds, taking things in, she plopped an armful of boxes and things down, drank some water, pulled a scribbled note card from her pocket, and looked at it – Dr Donovan Tryent, Psychologist. She would call him tomorrow to make an appointment for the grief counselling her family almost insisted she get. She stumbled upon him when researching Gig Harbor and then ventured off into therapists just to test the waters and read reviews on his website that he was 'Amazing'. He had a friendly face that she remembered.

"And also," she said as she looked up at the ceiling and around, "I need to get a dog. It's too damn quiet in here." And she smiled, then continued to fetch her things inside from the storage unit and her car until the sun went down.

Three

It was dark outside now and the lights worked just fine in the house. She had managed to get the things she needed inside and a few furniture pieces for the living room; a small table and chair. She had always prided herself in being a self-sufficient woman. She had learned to be creative moving heavy furniture in her single days and she knew how to get things done on her own if she needed to. She rather liked the quiet, alone with her thoughts after endless visits from fellow mourners. She didn't have to put on a face for anyone if she felt terrible. It was a relief. Someone who lost their husband should be allowed to fall apart, but somehow everyone needed to see that she was keeping it together. It wasn't fair, and it was a pressure a survivor shouldn't have to face. Moving was the perfect escape. The kitchen had her tea and coffee pot, a few pans, and some mugs and glasses.

She brought in the essential snacking items like chips for a nice cozy cuddle session with a book in her bed, or should she say, mattress, which was currently on the floor in the living room. She hadn't connected the bed frames in her room yet to receive the mattress. In fact, she hadn't even seen her room yet. Connecting bed frames was always like learning how to figure out a Rubik's cube, but she was confident the next day she would be clear-headed enough to get the job done. For now, her mattress and box spring lay on the floor of her living room, next to the fireplace, a lamp on the table and a single chair.

Although most people would feel a little scared sleeping in such a big house alone in such a wide-open space as it was, she had stopped being afraid of the dark since she was a little girl. She had stopped believing that her stuffed animals could move on their own when she wasn't there, or in the dark, and she started believing that those sounds in the night were simply old houses settling or animals outside moving about. Boxes lay scattered on the floor, and some food to make a sandwich had been brought in. She had carried boxes into the house as long as she could, before it got dark and placed them in the rooms they would be in, but she had not yet ventured upstairs. She was too exhausted and although moving had an excitement, she was always reminded in the moment of stagnation that her husband was dead and she was alone, no, worse, lonely. The ache would return, and the pain would be silencing to her. It got into her bones so deep she had to just wait for the pain to pass. In those moments, she herself died a little death before she could carry on. Every part of her body would lose energy and all she wanted to do, or could do, was roll up into a ball in her bed, piling covers around her to shut out the world and metaphorically, her pain. But it always failed. She couldn't run away from her pain and so she would deal with it a little at a time in measures she could handle. It had been

Sufani Weisman-Garza

months now and each month she was getting stronger and braver to move on. She had entered a new year without Clay, and it made her need to change, no, to accept her new life, all the more real. Life stripped her of her man, but in moments of despair Jo had a certain fire that welled up from the core of her being. She often felt life should come with a leather strap to bite down on to get through all the shit, pain and disappointment. But she also felt it should come with a glass jar filled with endless quotes of optimism, because the truth was that life would always become what your attitude was. She was choosing to move on and be grateful for what she had. She was not a wallower. Sitting on the edge of her bed the pain began to resurface and so she jumped up and went to the kitchen to make her dinner, a cold sandwich of Swiss cheese and roasted Tofurkey with fresh avocado. One could not complain. Her side for the evening, sour cream potato chips. She made her meal in no real hurry and went to the bed gripping the chip bag to her body like a child holding their favorite blanky. She had placed her comforter on the mattress and sat cross-legged, beginning to eat, as she surveyed the lay of the land.

She looked upward at the details of the ceilings. The rich crown molding was spectacular, surrounding all the rooms. Each extravagant chandelier in every room was encased by a medallion from times of old, breath-taking and something she had never seen up close before. Things could become so old that they were new again, and to her the house was filled with so much mystery and newness. So many pieces from an era she did not know but had all the time in the world to get acquainted with – and she planned on it. If there was anything that she had learned from the death of her husband, it was how fragile life was, and how much it made her want to live and not spend any time on nonsense. Even her career seemed littered with the insane routines of unnecessary dialogues and monotonous actions to achieve what? Paper in the wallet, status? Leaving her job was easy. She needed a change. Money was important, but for now it held no urgency to her, being that she had what she needed to take the time to heal. After so many thoughts and such a hard day, she finished her meal and found her eyes getting heavy; a clear sign to go to bed. It was already a little past ten according to her phone that seemed to be searching for service and then finding it. Tomorrow was a new day.

She stood on her mattress and got off momentarily to bring the lamp light down to the floor next to her. Positioning the light, she got cozy in bed again and had herself faced toward the rather large window that faced outside, as the moon came in and could still be seen through the sheer drapes. The heavy velvet drapes looked as regal as the house, gorgeous and layered. Although clearly not original, they were beautifully preserved. The home itself was a piece of art. The chair's back was against the rays of the moon shining in and she, facing the side

28

fireplace, felt ready to close her eyes. Within moments of looking outside, lost in the moonlight and her thoughts, she drifted into sleep.

Hours passed and she awoke, taking a moment to realize where she was, having no clue what time it really was and her phone was somewhere in the dark. She took a deep breath and was not surprised that she wasn't yet totally comfortable in her new place. It's normal to not be comfortable at first, especially when all the signs of home are still packed away. She got up to go to the bathroom, guided only by the moonlight that got increasingly less as she went toward the back bathroom at the end of the hall. Once inside, she had light. She could have turned on the lights in the hall, but she didn't want to. She also wasn't sure yet where they were.

Turning the light off in the bathroom she started down the hall, with her fingertips touching the walls of the hallway and the wooden banister of the staircase for balance, until she safely returned back to her mattress on the floor. She was somewhat blinded from the bathroom light into the total abyss of darkness, save for the sliver of light from the moon. She snuggled back into bed. As she did when she first got into bed, she was drawn to look toward the window into the light. As she rested her head softly on the pillow listening to the gentle creaks of the house the silent night fell over her and she gazed at the branches of the enormous -old tree, with its branches

29

peeking into the window from outside. She watched the wind blow the branches to and fro and began to feel the heaviness of her eyes once again. She began to close her eyes, enjoying the sound of the owls outside. Perhaps they were cooing and hooting to the light of the full moon?. The bed felt so comfortable and the pillow supporting her neck felt better than it had for months. She felt herself letting go and finally relaxing. Her eyes began to burn with dreams of sleep and to her right something caught her eye. She was beginning to see things the way a person sees shapes in a cloud. She began to fall asleep, forgetting the silly shape until the imagined shape in the dark startled her by moving. It was a shadow sitting in the chair facing her. She strained to make out what her eyes began to see take form. It was a man and she could see his arm moving a pipe into his mouth with his legs crossed in the chair.

"What the fuck?" she let out, shocked and frightened, as she fumbled for the lamp. Grasping for the switch she clumsily turned it on and looked up in the starkness of the light, jumping from her mattress, only to find an empty chair. Her heart was pounding out of her chest and she was scared half to death at the prospect of a stranger invading her home, but then the rush of irritation overcame her at getting so upset over nothing. How could she have just done that to herself? It was ridiculous! What just happened? Her eyes must have played a trick on her. Perhaps it was the stress of the move, or for that matter,

30

everything else?

She walked to the kitchen and got a drink of water and took a deep breath as she passed through the dining room to get back into her bed once again. Still a little frightened, she turned out the light, staring directly at the chair, feeling stupid doing it. The light went out and her eyes adjusted to the dark. All was still and she breathed nervously. She stared at the tree and the wind continued to blow its branches to and fro. The owls continued their singing, and the tapestries of the French drapery in the window maintained their beauty even in the pale light of the moon. Her heart had slowed its heavy beating, and the night again was still. The softness of her sheets and pillow again caressed her head and her shoulders sank into the bed lavishly. She closed her eyes for a good night's sleep but the temptation to open them kept her from dropping off. Closing them while awake, like a child faking to their mother they were asleep, she could not help herself. She opened her eyes and again from the side of her eye she saw the same figure, this time facing her directly in the chair. It struck a match, lighting what in shadow looked like a pipe. She let out a yell and this time hit the lamp, almost knocking it over. The sheer terror of being in the dark with this shadow figure made her movements sharp enough to catch the lamp before it hit the ground. She turned the light on again and, again, nothing was there. Her eyes creased and her chest was visibly rising and falling.

Sufani Weisman-Garza

1377 Rikoppe Lane

"What is this?" she yelled out angrily, standing on her mattress, staring at the chair, trying to see in the light what she saw in the moonlight. Her head darted around the room in every direction to see anything resembling a figure. Thunder struck outside out of nowhere and heavy drops of rain began to slap the windows making a loud noise. The owls were no longer cooing. After many minutes she sat back down on her mattress with the light on, never taking her eyes off the chair. She recounted the incident over and over again in her head as she stared at the empty chair. Although she saw the movements of a match being struck in the dark, there had been no flame. It was like watching a black and white movie, no color, just the familiar motions of someone lighting a pipe while sitting in a chair. Surely it happened; it was not her imagination, not twice. She spent hours sitting and staring at the chair until sleep and terror took over her consciousness. She woke to the light of day lying down on her mattress, still facing the chair. Exhausted and confused.

Sufani Weisman-Garza

Four

After lying in bed for a few moments staring at the trees outside, rain gone and beams of sun coming in the living room through the sheer drapes that hung in the center, her eyes burned from the lack of comforting sleep. She began thinking of the night before and her eyes wandered over to the chair that didn't look all that scary in the light of day. She began to laugh and snicker to herself. "Chsh … what an idiot," she said out loud and got up from the mattress laughing at herself for being so scared her first night in her big home. "That was totally my imagination," she said shaking her head to herself. With that acknowledgement, she continued to get ready for the day and the movers that she had arranged from town would be there in two hours or so. She gave them until 10am to start, not feeling that she had any need to rush her move in. Of course, she wanted her things in place, but she needn't flurry around like a crazy person to get it done. She had no deadlines or work to return to in a short period of time, so she could take her sweet time and that sounded just right to her. After her uneventful shower in the downstairs bathroom, with no Norman Bates sneaking into her bathroom unexpectedly, she got ready and made herself presentable. Clay entered her mind and no sooner did he arrive than she pushed him back out. No time for that today. Shower, shine and get ready for the day. That

33

was the plan. She'd cried enough for years of tears and just didn't want to do it anymore. She was all cried out; but her heart ached silently, and her memories were ruthless.

She opened the front door and the cold air came in like an uninvited guest. She had to get ready to start moving in some things on her own. The sky was gray. The coffee was brewing. She got her keys and unlocked the storage container door in the driveway. Looking over her things deciding what was first, she took a moment to pull a card out of her pants pocket. Dr Donovan Tryent, the card read. She thought to herself, she should call right away before people come. It would be nice to meet someone from town, even if it was a shrink. Beggars couldn't be choosers. She removed the cell phone from her back pocket and made the call. After asking for the appointment and being booked, she was surprised to have his assistant transfer her to speak to him directly. Small harbor towns really were different.

"Oh," she said surprised, "OK, great." The call was transferred, and a nice voice answered on the other end.

"Hello," the voice said as if he knew it was her. His voice was unpretentious.

"Oh, hello," she responded. "My name is Johannah Williams. I would like to book an appointment with you." There was silence, so she continued. "I'm new in town." She stopped herself and laughed for a moment. "Jesus, this sounds like a speed date." And she heard laughter on the other line.

"So, you're funny?" he responded and allowed a silent pause that she could only imagine was filled with a smile on his face. "My name is Donovan Tryent. My patients just call me Dr D if that is comfortable to you?"

"Oh, that's cute," she said. "OK, that sounds great. I already booked the time for tomorrow, you had a cancellation … lucky me," she said teasing. Again, he laughed with her.

"Alright then, I'll see you tomorrow," he said and they said their goodbyes and hung up. She found herself comforted by that small interaction and was looking forward to her meeting with him. It would be good to talk and he seemed friendly and pleasant. He didn't know her and to not be greeted with grieving was refreshing. That simple greeting made her feel normal and she needed that.

Five

Standing outside, after a few minutes surveying all the items in her storage, she turned around and looked at the house once more. She had more of a relationship with the house now than she did yesterday. It had scared her last night, but she knew it was just her nerves and being alone in a new house; a house with unfamiliar bumps in the night. She had been under a lot of strain with the death of her husband, the sale of her home and purchase of a new one in a new state. In a matter of months, her life had changed drastically. It was no wonder she was a little freaked out the night before. She realized as she looked up at the big windows of the front bedrooms that she had not yet even seen what was upstairs. There had been no time since she had arrived to even think about a lazy tour of the house. She was in a hurry to get things situated before night fall and once done, had been exhausted. Now that she had all day, she thought it prudent to go upstairs. Her eyes were drawn to the front room in the house, upstairs on the right. It had a nice big window and an old-fashioned deck just outside the center window between the two bedrooms to place some flowers in. It was sweet.

Hmm, she thought to herself as she began to look away, thinking of what flower or plant would be best there, when suddenly a shadow caught in her periphery drew her gaze back to the window on the right as she took in a

36

surprised breath. But it was gone.

"What was that?" she said out loud. She looked around and then away from the house into the sky to see what could have cast a shadow on the window, but she saw nothing. The sun beams were shining through minimal patches of morning fog. She crinkled her face and scratched her head, confused. She thought to herself, it must have been a bird flying by and just then she heard a rustling in the tree by the house and a crow flew out and across the way to another tree. That's what it was. She would have to get used to all the wildlife by her house. It would take time. In the meantime, she would work on being less jumpy about everything. She thought it would probably be a good idea to take a tour of the upstairs, before the movers showed up, so she could guide them where to put specific things as they moved them in. It would make it harder if she had to move all the boxes around herself once brought inside.

She walked back inside the entry way and closed the door. She left the storage unit out front open, not having any trepidation of thievery. Somehow, Gig Harbor did not put off the vibe that you had to lock everything if you stepped out of sight for a moment. Not like other places. She walked down the ominously long hallway and a memory of the night before came over her, giving her a feeling of an inner, silent creepiness that she did not want to acknowledge. This was her home, and she could not feel uncomfortable in it already. This was the bonding time. Besides, the night before was all in her imagination anyway, so all of that was just silly regardless. Anyone in her position would feel jumpy and out of sorts with her current situation and what she had been through. Seeing the therapist would be cathartic for her.

She went to the back hall staircase for some reason instead of entering it from the front and made a right-hand U-turn, taking the first step and looking up to the second floor, as it creaked. She smiled; it was cute the way the house seemed to play up to all the stereotypes of an old Victorian home. She continued up the stairs, introduced to the comfortable landing with a cute little maid station for linens, and behind it against the wall a beautifully ornate large wall cabinet for more storage quite different from the other and was confronted again by another long hallway that led to all the bedrooms; four on the right and one on the left. The walls were lined with velvet wallpaper, hardwood floors with expensive, old fashioned hallway rugs and a large heavily draped window in between the last two rooms, again with a sheer curtain in the center like the living room to allow light in at the end of the hall.

Two bedrooms were in shadow off to the right and slightly behind the staircase. Instead of viewing those first she went into the third bedroom on the right, just passed where the staircase landing left you. She would circle back to the others later. The third room had its own internal short hall off to the right that led to a large bathroom with an old-fashioned claw tub. There was a large closet on the left just before the hallway leading to the bathroom with French doors and French blinds from ceiling to floor in hardwood concealing its inside. To the left was a wall for the bed and on the far wall a nice fireplace. Directly opposite the door leading into the room there was a window overlooking the water from the harbor and some trees. It was I so pretty. There were assorted pieces of antique furniture already left in the room to be used. The hall as well as the room was decorated in mauve velvet wallpaper; creating a soft feminine feeling that calmed the spirit.

"Lovely," she said to herself and walked back into the hall for the next room on the right. A large bay window large enough to put a lounging chair for afternoon naps, or reading a book, with a floor lamp with a crystal shade and tassels, hanging over the chair and a small table, all facing out just catching a glimpse of the community and landscape. She surmised now that all the rooms would have some furniture still left in them and it was welcomed. This room had a smaller fireplace to the left, kitty corner to the window. Because the space and window were rounded out, it did not take away any space in the rest of the room. The rest of the room was quite large with the far wall being partly where the headboard of a bed would go, facing the window, and to the right of where the bed would go another window, six feet or so, going all the way to the floor with French blinds up to the ceiling. Up high, behind where the bed would go, was a stained glass window that clearly was part of the bathroom. A short walk from the bed was a special room made for a sink and to its right, a floor to ceiling curio closet that was built into the wall. Large wooden doors opened up and although it looked as if it would be just a relatively average closet, its depth was surprising—like trick architecture. Although it was unnoticeable from the room, in the hall there was a curve that gave signs of how they created the space. Quite amazing, she thought to herself.. The next room across from the one she had just come out of and on the left was similar to the last, but a little smaller and did not have the little something special the other rooms had. It had a fireplace kitty corner to the window facing the front of the house, but it did not have a bay window. In every way, the room was as beautiful, but it was dark in areas, felt colder and damper somehow. Perhaps it was from not having the sun come in the windows the same way as the other room? It too had a large curio cabinet built into the wall at a different angle to accommodate the flush of the wall, having no hallway to build in to. It was probably the reason the room was a tad bit cozier. Trees in front no doubt blocked more of the light than the other rooms.

The bathrooms were identical in architecture but not in style. She flipped on the light to the bathroom

40

revealing a tub, with black and mauve Victorian tiles where the stained glass was in the master bedroom across the hall, high up on the wall. The same tile was manifest on the back wall to which the tub lay horizontal. It was beautiful but felt heavier in mood. Where the other rooms felt cheerful, this one felt a bit macabre. Dark mahogany wood was used in all furniture pieces in the bathroom, sink and curio. The other room's furniture pieces had been painted white, with gold leafing and felt more pleasant. This room gave her a chill and she exited it not yet having opened the walk-in curio closet, although her eyes continually were drawn to that dark corner of the room. She looked back at it as she stood in the doorway, considering walking back to open it, but was interrupted by the movers pulling in the driveway behind her car and the rather large storage unit. She ran over to the window as the men were getting out of their truck. One of the men glanced at her as she cranked the window open and yelled out, "I'll be right down," and smiled. The mover acknowledged her waving with a smile and nod. She closed the window and the door to that room behind her, sprinted to the other two rooms and peeked her head in to see two more lovely similar rooms as the ones she already investigated, and hurried downstairs to greet her movers and began her new life.

Six

She pulled into the parking lot of the doctor's office building to start her grief counselling. It would be good to talk. She parked and entered the building, finding suite 113 as was written on her paper. Inside it was a warm and friendly environment with a mature woman at the front desk who stood and greeted her as she entered.

"Hello! You must be Mrs. Williams?"

She smiled a sad smile and said, "Yes," thinking she was no longer a Mrs. anymore. "You can just call me Jo," she said to the woman and smiled slightly.

"Of course," the woman responded. "Here is some paperwork to fill out," she said and handed her the expected forms on a clipboard.

"OK," she said looking through to see how many there were. She wasn't fond of filling out papers at doctors' offices. They never looked at or read them anyway it seemed. You'd fill everything out and then the doctor would come in holding the paperwork and ask you all the same questions all over again. Seemed tedious to her; a flaw in the process that could be updated.

"My name is Lucy," the doctor's assistant said smiling. "If you need anything, or have a question, don't hesitate to ask," and she sat back down resuming her work on charts.

"Thank you," Jo responded looking up briefly. When she was done with the paperwork, she brought it back to

Lucy.

"Alright, dearie, the doctor will be right out," she said smiling at Jo and looking her in the eyes and then down to the paperwork to make sure everything was in order. Just then the doctor came out of his office and walked up, next to Lucy. She seemed surprised. "Oh! Well, Doctor, this is your next patient, Johannah!" and she smiled and handed the doctor the clip board. He smiled at Jo and quickly opened the door to the back office area for her to come through.

"Right this way," he said opening the door for her and then the short walk to the next door, opening that for her as well. He was a gentleman and had a kind-hearted, soft energy, without saying much. Good breeding and manners, Jo surmised. And not bad looking either. In fact, very good looking. He had a very Keanu Reeves handsomeness you could not escape, masculine, sensitive, well dressed but not overly so.

"Thank you," she said as she entered through both doorways. He followed her.

"Have a seat here," he said pointing to the lovely Robert Adam style chair, with teal tapestry and gold leaf. The entire room was full of the same style furniture, very elegant in style, yet comfortable. There was a matching loveseat, another chair with a black and teal pattern that was the doctor's chair next to a side table with the necessary tools for writing and such. There were two

43

matching mahogany demilune commodes that were much like sofa tables, flush on one side to place against a wall or couch. One was against the wall in the entrance and one directly behind the loveseat. The room had a darker teal color on the wall with mahogany-colored drapes with gold accents tying the whole room together. Each piece of furniture and decoration seemed carefully chosen for its uniqueness. It was comforting and soft, although regal at the same time. He had good taste – really good taste – and that surprised her. She was happy knowing that she would be coming there for a while to talk to the doctor. She approached it much more like a social visit than a need for psychotherapy.

"Beautiful place you have here," she said looking into his eyes, as he took a seat in his chair.

"Thank you. I like to decorate a bit. I love it so much more when you pick each individual piece for a room. I'm not much for catalogue ordering. I like to see the furniture and hand pick it, one piece at a time." He smiled as though a little uncomfortable that he went on too much about himself. "Anyway, let's talk about you," he said and folded his hands in his lap and settled into his chair. "First, would you like some water or tea?"

"Oh, no, thank you. I'm fine," she said.

He nodded. "So, I have read the notes in your file and remember from talking with you briefly on the phone, why you are here. I am very sorry for your loss."

She said nothing, just looked down and nodded, crinkling her mouth on one side, almost exhausted by the phrase, but understanding it was all one could say to her to acknowledge her 'situation'. She looked up. "So how does this work? Where do I start?"

"Most people start from now and go backwards. It's easier. But there's no set way, it's all up to you."

"OK, well, my sister and mother suggested that I go to a doctor to get some grief counselling. I believe in talking, I think it's a good way to let it all out," she said using her arms to express the release. "I feel like I'm doing okay, considering. If you saw me in the beginning, you would see the difference."

"Oh?" the doctor replied.

She smiled. "Yes, the word zombie comes to mind," and she let out a small laugh almost to herself. His smile in return to her was one of compassion.

"Go on."

"Well, as you know I am new here and I needed to get away, so I decided to start over somewhere else and here I am." She looked at him with the look that she had given him the whole story.

He smiled. "Aha, and so what was it you needed to get away from exactly?"

She smiled. "Good question, Doctor D!" She looked around the room at the drapes and continued, "Well, for one, the *constant* apologies for my loss. I understand it, it's

Sufani Weisman-Garza

natural for people to say it, but I just couldn't keep being the grief spawn. It just seemed like if I stayed there, I would constantly be reminded of Clay's suicide, not only by familiarity of the setting, but also by the sad looks in people's eyes every time they'd see me. Because of how Clay died, there is also shame."

"You feel shame?" the doctor asked.

"Oh, no, not me. But in general, it is a shame that someone takes their own life and people understand that there is shame in dying like that. It's a question mark you see in everyone's eyes, mixed with compassion. I just didn't want to be around that all the time." She got up and walked around the room. "Overcoming Clay's death and having to endure people saying sorry to me for God knows how long?" she said not finishing the statement. She spun the world globe that was placed on the sofa dune and looked up. "The house was not something I wanted to stay in either. I had always felt it was Clay's place. The style was his and it felt a little cold to me. Then when he was gone, it *really* felt cold. Besides, who in the world would continue to stay in a house where their loved one hanged themselves in the closet? I couldn't even be in that room anymore."

"Oh!" he said.

"Yah, I believe that things hold energy. Like the room. It held on to the sadness that made Clay do what he did. Kind of how you like to pick out the furniture by seeing

46

and touching it first! Everything carries energy to it. The energy of the furniture tells a story." She looked at him for confirmation.

"I see, continue," he said, understanding her meaning, his legs crossed, holding a pen and a pad lying in his lap.

She smiled that he understood about energy. It was important to her. So many people walk around denying that everything is connected in that way. It meant a lot to her that her doctor was evolved enough to get the simplest of things that most people seem to miss.

"So I just moved all my things out and never went back in there. I made plans shortly after the burial to move out once I found a new house. It brought me here."

"And how did you settle on Gig Harbor?" he asked.

"A random Google search, actually," she said whimsically. "I just found it and looked at pictures and video and decided. I felt good about it. We had a realtor already who was aware of what was going on and I had him help pick out a new place here. I told him what I wanted, a Victorian, and he found one for me." She stopped and looked at him. "It's up the winding road by the harbor on Rikoppe Lane. You know it?"

His eyebrows went up. "Oh, yes, of course. It's very nice up there and spacious. I live in that area as well, a few streets away from you." He smiled, of course not giving away his street name, which would be ill advised. For all he knew, she could turn out to be a psycho and then he'd have a real problem on his hands.

She shook her head quickly several times and lifted her eyebrows as well. "Oh. Great," and she smiled. "You do house calls?"

He laughed, knowing she was kidding. "No, not usually," he said softly. "Now, tell me about this venture with your new home. How did your first few nights go?"

"Well," she said with her voice and energy changing, "good, good," which sounded more like she was thinking about something.

The doctor's eyes and mouth scrunched together inquisitively.

She responded. "The house, of course, is new to me and makes a lot of settling noises, and I am a bit jumpy from being new to it and of course alone in a big house. All my things were not unpacked the first night. I got there just before nightfall so there was a mismatch of comforts available to me. I think that made me not sleep so well and see things."

A look of concern came over his face. "See things?"

She waved him off. "Oh, nothing really. Not like schizophrenia — see things, like shadows and such. I was looking at the moonlit night trying to fall asleep and thought I saw a shadow in the chair." She looked at him and his eyebrows again went up. "I turned on the light and there was nothing there. It was just me being tired and nervous in a new place." She shrugged it off. "I was terrified, though, at the time," she said, while the slight remembrance of that night chilled her bones. "It felt like an intruder was in my home. I was quite scared, actually," she said with a distant look and then at the doctor, laughing under her breath. "Silly though," she said with a smile. "Just first night jitters and getting used to everything."

"Well, you have been through considerable stress and changes that are enough to put anyone on edge. I want to caution you; reduce your stress during this time and focus on more relaxing things. Bring things into your home that make you feel comfortable. Put night lights in around the house to avoid those little scares from being in a new home and go out and meet some neighbors. We have a farmers' market every Saturday and Sunday from nine to one on Tesh Street. Go shopping and meet some of your neighbors. You need to feel connection to a new community. Go eat at a few diners and get to know the restaurants that make you feel like you have places to stop at for connection. Isolation is the last thing you need. Also, do you have family that you are close with?"

She smiled. "Yes, my annoying sister who actually was the one who pushed this very hard on me. But I haven't called her yet or told her where I live," she said with a smirk. "She's gonna be so mad at me, but I needed a breather. She can be a little smothering; all for good but I wanted a few days from her. I mean, she knew I was moving out of state and which state, just not the actual address. I told her I'd call her in a few days."

The doctor's expression of concern changed to ease, and he understood the obvious playful dynamic of her and her sister. "I see. Well, call your sister and have her come visit. The new needs a bit of the old to feel balanced. Will you do that for me?" he asked.

"Yes, of course, doctor. I was planning on it anyway."

"We'll start up next visit by talking more about Clay. We didn't speak too much about the incident today, but what happened around him. I think it will be prudent to go into that if you're up to it next visit. There is probably much there that needs to be released. You can start with how you met, and we'll move forward. Next week then?"

She nodded her head, and her eyes got a little heavy. "Yes, there is, and sounds good!" she said knowingly. "Well, this was a good first visit. I didn't really know what to expect, but I actually liked this. Thanks, Doc," and she reached out to shake his hand.

He shook her hand gently, but not too softly, and said goodbye. "Lucy automatically rolls patients weekly in the same time slot, so if you need to change it, let her know up front, okay?"

"OK, but next week this time is good for me."

They both smiled and he walked her through his office door to the next one and waved goodbye. He returned to his office and closed the door. She said goodbye to Lucy and told her she would see him again same time next week and left. As she walked out of the office and into the parking lot, she thought to herself how light she felt. It was good to talk to someone, even if just to share the daily things. It was one of the things she used to do with Clay that ended so abruptly, and it was good to do it again. She smiled.

Sufani Weisman-Garza

Seven

After her appointment with the doctor, she felt better and spent the next few days unpacking and arranging the house. She was feeling more at peace in her own space. She had given considerable attention to her room, and it was about finished. She had purchased period pieces to go with her new Victorian home mixed with pieces left in the house, even some in the basement, a very scary space, and the house began to take on the feeling of a time in the world not her own. It felt wonderful to be in this space and time, and it made her feel alive again, but as a new person. She had begun to work on the bedroom before her own and had already addressed the kitchen, living room and library where she set up her desk and began to unpack all her books from their boxes. She had always been an avid reader and needed many book shelves to hold them all. But the house came equipped with built-in shelving in the library, so she had made arrangements to put her bookshelves in the long hallway to fill up the long, lonely space. They were hardwood and were floor to ceiling shelves with borders. They were amazing and she could not part with them. She knew that in time even the massive built-in library shelves would fill up with books and she would need more space. It was always her dream to one day pass on to her children, who would one day have their own library. These of course were dreams of the future.

One she had thought she would have fulfilled with Clay, but now tucked it away as a dream that she thought no further about then the book itself. Simply to have them in her presence made her feel safe and not alone. She thought to herself, I better call my sister. She punched in her number. The phone was answered on the first ring and Layce was already talking.

"Oh my God, you are so dead!" the voice chastised.

"Hello, Layce. How are you, my dear sister?" she said with a playful sarcasm.

"Jo Jo, seriously, I'm telling Mommy. That is really messed up to not tell me where you are all this time and to not answer any of my five hundred calls to you. For all I knew, you were dead on the side of a road or something."

"Well, here I am, very much alive to take your beating, thank you very much."

A deep sigh was let out on the other end of the phone and Layce continued with a happy demeanor – apparently all was forgiven. "OK, tell me everything. How is it there? Do you like it, have you met anyone there yet, what's the town like, is it too quiet, or just right?"

"Jesus, Layce!"

"Your problem!" she said unapologetically for accosting her sister with questions. "You were the one who didn't call me, so unfortunately for you, you get all my questions condensed."

"Okay. Yes, I like it very much, although I haven't seen

too much of it yet. The town has a nice old feel too it, community like, friendly, but also a private feeling — you know, people say hello, but they don't get into your business. I met the movers and the doctor and his assistant."

"Whoa, you met a doctor? What does that mean — for psychiatric help, right?"

"Layce, I don't think I'm quite ready to date just yet," she said correcting her insinuation that she would be looking for men to date. It had only been months since Clay was gone and she hadn't even dealt with all her pain yet.

"Yes, I'm sorry, Sis," Layce said apologetically, acknowledging the seriousness of her sister's pain. "I know. I'm just enthusiastic for you is all, but I understand. I'm sorry."

Johannah smiled quietly to herself. Even though her sister was flighty, spirited, so uncontrollably happy and enthusiastic at all times that it annoyed her, she was also loyal, adorable, loving, caring and made her feel needed. "I love you, Layce," she said to her.

"I love you too — when can I come out?" she asked back-to-back with no breaks for air. "I'll request a few days off and come help you with whatever. Just tell me when."

"I'll look at tickets for you and plan maybe; I don't know Tuesday or Wednesday. I know Monday is too soon for you."

"No, it isn't, let's do it for Monday. A few girls owe me for covering for them, so I know I can get it off."

"Are you sure, Layce, that you can get off that soon? It's only three days away and you said the massage therapists don't always cover for you."

"Yes, positive," Layce responded.

"Okay, I'll get your ticket for you tonight and email the details, Sis." Jo had always flipped the bill for her little sister. She always had more money and Layce felt almost like a child to her in some ways. Layce was bohemian and her money was funny, up, and down from the massage business becoming saturated with twenty-dollar foot massages everywhere that rub your back and shoulders. People didn't want to pay full prices anymore according to Layce, so her business was up and down. Jo didn't resent helping her sister. She was happy to do it and never thought twice about it. Layce gave her support in return and loyalty beyond what anyone could ever expect. She appreciated that.

"Awesome!" Layce said drawing out the word and Jo just knew she was bobbing her head and doing a happy dance on the other end of that phone. Everything Layce did or said was animated.

"Have you talked to Mom?" Jo asked.

"Yes, daily. I had to talk to someone since you wouldn't pick up my calls. She wasn't mad at you at all."

Jo had taken more after her mother than Layce had.

Layce wasn't even like their late father. Milk man was the only conclusion. "Yes, of course, Mom understood I needed some alone time, but knew I would eventually call."

"Well," she said letting the word drift off into silence. "Anyway, give me your address right now. I don't trust you!"

Johannah gave her the information and told Layce she would talk with their mother as well and buy her a ticket to come out too, but after Layce's arrival, so they had some sister time just them. Mom would come out a few days later to stay for a few days. They disconnected the line and she felt like some balance had been restored to her. It didn't feel right to isolate herself from family. That was passed for her now.

Although she had begun decorating many of the rooms, arranging furniture and placing personal items in every space, the only room she had not touched was the one across from her bedroom. She had decorated even the room in the hall before hers. It was so lovely already with beautiful wallpaper and drapes that it only needed the right furniture placement to come alive. But something in the other room, the room across from hers, felt so different and for some reason she had not felt ready to take on that particular room. It was darker, colder, and gave her a sort of anxious feeling she couldn't quite place. Perhaps she would save that room as a little project for she and Layce

56

to tackle. It would be a good scheme to work on together. Yes, she decided, that was a great idea, that's what they would do together. After she got off the phone with Layce, she got ready for the farmer's market. She used to go to the farmers' market occasionally in Huntington Beach and always liked it, but found that she and Clay just seemed too busy between the two careers to make the commitment to go regularly. Plans always seemed to be interrupted by unexpected work phone calls and choices for the more convenient and fast solution to food usually took precedence. Jobs with big salaries also came with big interruptions and hassles. She wanted to change things now that she had time to get consistent in a new pattern and figured that shopping at the farmers' market was a great way to get to see and possibly know a few neighbors, or, at minimum, local farmers and suppliers. It was literally a few blocks from her house in the parking lot of the harbor docking area and so she grabbed her keys to lock up, her purse, a few cloth bags and slipped on her Vans and off she went.

She walked out the door and for some reason, every time she walked away from the house, she always felt she needed to look back, her eyes were always drawn to the upstairs window of the room she hadn't touched. Seeing nothing but darkness in the room she turned around and made her way off to the farmers' market. She could see up ahead the hustle and bustle of a happy community doing their shopping, parking, walking, talking, and others passing her on the street, nodding hello with their bags of produce. She, saying hello and being cheerful to all her new neighbors and community friends. The air had become chilly now that the weather was getting colder. They had even had some earlier morning drizzle and the day was a bit grey with moments of light and blue sky breaking through the gloom. Still, in the breezy market, people went about their business of picking arugula, beets, and broccoli. She found herself at a stand picking out green leaf kale and romaine and found her way to the organic cremini mushrooms. While sorting through some and placing them in her plastic bag, she happened to look out toward the water to take in the beauty of her new neighborhood. To her surprise, across the way was Dr Donovan. He was looking straight at her with a smile, holding green onions in his hand. He waved his free fingers to acknowledge her. She put up a finger as to say, one moment, and she paid for her items. She walked over to say hello. "Hey, Dr D. Good to see you!"

"Good to see you too!" he replied politely. She noticed he looked so much more at ease and kind of cute in his light-colored jeans and white cotton sweater. He also had on Vans, something she immediately admired. Vans were such a beach and harbor person's shoe. Easy on, easy off.

"Good to see you getting out and seeing the

58

neighborhood. It's a little chilly in the morning though. Next time you might want to wear a light jacket, or sweater." And he pointed at her short sleeve shirt. "It can get breezy this close to the water."

"Yes, you're right, I was just noticing that on the walk over. So, you really do live near me. I walked here. You?" she asked.

"No, I drove. I'm a little farther out, but I could walk here. It would just take fifteen minutes or so to get here. I should have, actually, but didn't," he said a little embarrassed.

She noticed he was alone. She looked around. "Came by yourself?"

He just nodded yes and smiled. His brown hair gently blew across his forehead. "Ah, so I will see you this coming week?" he asked to insert something into the awkward silence and smiles.

"Yes," she said with a quiet giggle and looked down. "Oh, and I called my sister, you'll be happy to know. She and my mother are coming out to visit this week too, so they officially know where I am." She smiled at him, and he smiled back saying it was good that she called them. "Well, I'm gonna finish up here and get back home. I still have so much to do to make it mine, you know?"

He smiled, said okay and waved and gave a friendly smile goodbye. "See you soon," he said, and they went on with their shopping in different directions.

It was nice to see the doctor out. He was a warm sort of guy. She noticed no wedding ring and of course doctors have to be reticent about their personal life to patients. Although she was not looking at him as her sister Layce would be, she thought highly of him and liked being around him. He was warm in an unspoken way, and it felt nice being in his presence. Even in multiple locations, he was consistently the same man. That was a gift in a person, she felt. So many people are not the same in every situation and very inconsistent people. It was nice to see more of who he was, and it helped her to feel comfortable telling him the personal details of her life. It just made it easier to take advice from someone she liked and looked up to. She walked home from the market with her bag of perishables for the week. There was even a fresh pastries stand at which she bought a large homemade brownie and some sweet rolls to have with her tea in the afternoon. She walked home pleasantly lost in her thoughts and wondered how Clay would have liked it. She imagined what it would be like to walk with him down her street, holding hands and talking. But the truth was that he had gotten so stressed and busy over the last two years that this move would have never occurred, and if they did have time to walk this way, he would be distracted and, on his phone taking phone calls for work non-stop unless he decided to simply ignore them, which he did on occasion.

Her work was busy but for the most part when she

60

went home it was her time. Clay's work was never that way. He ate, slept, and breathed his work. He had lost balance in his life as some people do. She thought how he must have believed that his job was his life, his identity, to do what he had done to himself. But his work was not who he was, it was what he did. He was a beautiful person, but under the pressure he became darker as time went on. That Clay was harder to be around. But still, she loved him dearly and always tried to shine light on him. Be the light of his day and life. She knew he was under stress, but she did not know how badly. He kept hard things away from her, he loved her that much. She knew he never wanted his stress to become hers, so he would just not tell her things. Ultimately, he didn't tell her what he was going through. She thought to herself, maybe if he did, he'd be here with her now. But she couldn't live in that thinking. She had to move on now. Live her life and keep him in living memories. She smiled and just thought of how he would like the weather and view, and she continued up to her driveway and took out her key to unlock the door to her stunning Victorian – a house bought with death money.

Sufani Weisman-Garza

Eight

She went to bed that night and loved that she could leave her French blinds open to see the moonlight shine in. Her view was unobstructed, and the view made her feel at peace. There was a lounge in front of the window to look out at the beautiful scenery of trees in the near distance. No smoking man had come so far to sprawl in her chair in front of her window. Her imagination had settled, as she began to bring her own things in the house and had gotten used to the noises of the house. She was excited for her mother and sister to be coming to visit her. As much as she was annoyed by them at times, she also knew she needed them in her life. It was a symbiotic relationship of acceptance of one's annoyances and love for the ridiculous. All of them in their way were quirky, the most being Layce who didn't care at all what other people thought. It was the character trait loved most by all who knew her.

Her eyes began to get heavy as she lay in bed thinking about her family and how much she loved them. When the picture of Clay's hanging body appeared in her mind, she quickly inserted the picture of them from a vacation, of their faces smiling and being happy. She could not have that picture of Clay in her mind. It was difficult to forget, but she made efforts daily to change that picture. She could not survive seeing that last image day in and day out. With beautiful pictures in her mind, the nightmare of the reality

62

subsided, and she fell asleep.

After what felt like hours of sleep, she woke up to creaking sounds and then heard a snapping sound. She sat up gently in bed and looked out her window. The moon was shining so brightly into her room, and she stood and went to the window, her white flowing nightgown sweeping across the hardwood floor as she walked. She stood behind the side curtains and held them back to see out without being seen. There was no one below that she could see. Then she saw on the ground a large branch from the tree had broken off. Instantly she knew that was the sound that had woken her up. Acknowledging this, she breathed in a soft sigh. She turned to return to the bed and as she did there was a dark silhouette of a young girl in complete darkness holding a doll by the arm as it hung by her side. Jo let out a frightened yelp, as the shadow moved closer to her. Instantly, her eyes bulged and she found she was looking at the ceiling. She sat up in bed, awakened by terror into her true reality. It was a dream. Was it a dream? It felt so real. She sat up in bed and put her hands over her face, heart pounding and breathing heavy.

"Oh, my God, that was so scary," she said to herself. She looked over to her door which was standing open, and she quickly got up to shut it. She was cold from being in shorts and a muscle shirt. After she closed the door, she walked over to the window, curtains tied back from never being let down, French blinds still in place and the moonlight was strong, just as it was in her dream. She looked out the window and down onto the lawn, looking for the snapped branch. It was not there. It was still there, healthy and attached. She took a deep breath and let it out just as hard. She was afraid to turn around, but did so bracing herself, and when she did, her door was still closed and the room was lit up brightly by the moon, so that all corners of the room could be seen. It was just a dream, a nightmare. There was no little girl in the corner of her room. She walked back to the bed and took a drink of water from her tumbler on the nightstand and climbed back in bed. She stared out the window finding it hard to resume sleep. She grabbed her phone from the nightstand, put on Pandora and entered nature sounds. Once it was on, she felt more relaxed. She got up out of bed one more time to lock her bedroom door and then climbed back in. Once she did, she eventually fell back to sleep, undisturbed by any more nightmares with creepy, shadowy little figures in the dark.

Nine

Johannah woke up and immediately got in the shower. She had decided somewhere between sleeping and getting out of bed that she was going to go get a dog today. Something big and intimidating that would act as her watch dog, patrolling the house at night and mostly just making her feel secure in such a big home. She had no idea where to go but had planned on just walking into the town and seeing what was out there and asking the locals where the nearest shelter was. She didn't want a puppy, she wanted a dog who was an adult which she didn't have to train to go to the bathroom, or anything like that. She would get a beast of a dog that would scare even a shadow, she had thought amusingly to herself in the shower. Ready to leave the room she grabbed her purse, unlocked her bedroom door, and was immediately greeted face-to-face by the door across from hers. It was an overcast day, but the kind that, although there was no sun, it was blindingly light with a silver sky.

Standing in the doorway of her bedroom looking at the other door, she got a strange feeling in her stomach. She looked to her right and looked out her immense bedroom window to see the tree bowing in the wind gently. It was a breezy, gray day. She looked back at the door across the hall again, still having not moved an inch. She looked at the door and could see that a beam of

65

breakthrough light had broken from behind the clouds and had filled that room as well from the light coming out from the bottom of the door. She smiled and stepped forward deciding to go in and take a look at the room. As she walked the two steps forward to reach the door, she extended her hand and noticed the light under the door become shaded for a moment, as though something walked by blocking out the light. She gasped and hesitated, but then opened the door right away. Looking out the window she saw the trees in front blowing in the wind just as she saw it in her room. It must have been one of the trees moving that temporarily blocked out the light. She thought to herself a moment and looked around at the floor.

"There better not be a fucking rat in here!" she said quickly, a little intimidated by the thought of free running rodents. She looked around and knelt down on the floor. Then, standing up, she said to herself, "I mean, I like rats but not just … running around. I have rules you know!" Her words had no real conviction. She had rules, mostly to be broken; she just wasn't a hard person. She bent rules all the time. She finished carrying on the conversation with herself and looked around the room again. She usually was eager to decorate a room or could easily be inspired to decorate in a certain style, but this room felt strange to her, unwelcoming in some weird way. It was beautiful, but still felt cold and dark, although the trimmings, style and architecture were the same as the other rooms. It was strange. She would add faux geraniums, a palm tree and some ferns to jazz and liven the room up. In fact, she would put some in all the bedrooms. It was a nice gesture to the house, being so old and alive with history. It would be a friendship offering. She loved high quality faux plants that looked good all year round and she couldn't kill them. For such a large home, she would have to hire someone to keep up all the plants if they were real. She loved a home filled with greenery.

A cold chill came over her and she decided to leave the room and head out. It was time to get a dog. She stepped out of the room and closed the door. She walked down the hall looking back once at the door, still seeing the bright silver light from outside beneath the door. She turned around and headed down the stairs. The silver light shined brightly from under the door into the hall, then blacked out for a longer moment than the first time and then returned as it was.

Sufani Weisman-Garza

Ten

Walking down the street she went into a shopping center just up a few blocks. It was such a nice neighborhood and she liked walking to places. People rarely did that anymore where she had lived. Even though it was a beach town, they lived further inland and so it became just like any other neighborhood that you drove everywhere to. It just had nicer air. But even that had been changing in Huntington Beach, with the population growing steadily. Gig Harbor still felt somewhat small town and she loved the way it felt. It was friendly.

She walked into a coffee shop simply called Mamma's. A big light in the window of a huge cup of coffee gave it away to anyone who may have not known what Mamma was selling. The few empty tables and chairs outside under the large awning made it obvious to all onlookers that it was a coffee shop. Even in the winter cold and rain, Washingtonians were out in it. She went inside and ordered a double soy cappuccino to go. After a few minutes, the barista called her name she gave as 'Jo' and she went to get her drink.

"Say," looking at the girl's name tag, "Ginni. Do you know where there is a dog shelter or humane society, something like that? I want to get a dog."

No sooner the words came out of her mouth Ginni was pointing to the left. "In the corner of this shopping

68

center, actually," she said, smiling.

"Oh, great!" she said with raised eyebrows. How easy this was becoming?

"Ask for Rico. He's my boyfriend. His name is Ricardo, but everyone calls him Rico. It means rich and generous in Spanish. He'll help you find the love of your life," she said and smiled at Jo and then went back to steaming milk.

"Thanks, Ginni." She started to walk away and then turned back. "I'm new here. You'll be seeing me more often," she said and smiled.

"That a warning?" Ginni said playfully while smiling and not even looking up. She was pleasant and a cross between serious and jolly, an interesting combination that worked. "See you soon, 'no longer a stranger'," she said and laughed to herself.

Johannah smiled and walked away saying thank you and waving to everyone there and walking out, and they waved back even though they were busy with their own business. They were friendly people. Down south they were friendly, but most would have not even have returned the wave or looked up for that matter. Life had gotten too busy in her estimation. People were losing their humanity in the interim.

"Now, to find a mutt," she said to herself as she walked in the direction of the corner of the shopping center that Ginni had pointed to. She walked left, armed with the name of Rico who was promised to help her. She looked at all the stores and so far, none of them looked very doggish. Then she came upon a spa and stopped. She looked up at the sign that read 'Ruff Times and Happy Endings'. The subtext on the sign said 'Transitional Love Spa for Dogs'. She felt an instant heart-warming feeling as she read the sign. Who was this dear person who created this place? she thought. And whoever did, did so with humor. The pun on spa and happy endings was clever, although Layce wouldn't appreciate it, being that she was a massage therapist and had sometimes dealt with disgusting men who would ask for their own happy ending. To be fair, though, Layce had also mentioned that she had heard of only one woman at the spa who asked for that from a male therapist. But she said that was extremely rare. She walked into the store and up to the front counter to the receptionist, who was a male and quite possibly who she was looking for.

"Is Rico here?"

"'Tis I," he said intelligently, as he was looking down at his work while standing behind the desk. He had thick black rimmed glasses that made him look very Cary Grant. He was wearing a white lab coat, had grey eyes and black silky hair, thick and shiny with a few loose curls. Probably late twenties or early thirties and she immediately thought of Ginni and how they must look very cute together. He looked up at her and she continued.

70

"Ginni sent me."

His eyes got bigger. "Oh, she did, did she?" he said inquisitively with the same air of joviality, and he smiled at her.

"Yes, indeed. And I am in the market to be saved by a rather large dog. I just moved in to the large Victorian down the street and would love to have a protector of sorts. Have you anyone that fits that bill?"

"Of course, we do," he said matter-of-factly and opened the thigh level flip door that clearly kept the dogs who were out of their cages from passing. He welcomed her to the back area. The half door wouldn't do much for the jumpers, but was more of a boundary for them, she thought to herself. They walked through another set of doors and there were large dog kennels on the left side and each had multiple dogs to play together. They seemed happy and had play toys and food and water. Everything in the room was sparkling clean, including the walls and there were soft colors and flowers set throughout the path on small tables. The dogs could see them, and she felt it was warm feeling and dog spa like. Slowly passing each kennel and looking in, Rico excused himself and said he would return, giving her some time to look on her own. She came upon a large Great Dane and said, "Hold the phone," as she stopped in front of his kennel. "Now you are what I am looking for," she said out loud. "Jesus, I could ride you as a horse too," she said looking at it. He looked at her with no particular interest. Then she was distracted by the noisy grunting and heavy breathing coming from the kennel next door. She leaned left to see what was making that obnoxious noise and saw three pudgy English Bulldogs play fighting with a rubber squeak toy, slobbering all over each other, body ramming and trying to move their stocky bodies around fast, which wasn't fast at all. She stepped over to look at them and they instantly ran up to her, one with the squeak toy in its mouth and dropped it in front of her. Then the dog looked down and jumped up an inch on its front feet and made a head gesture for her to pick it up.

"Well, I can't," she said. "There's a gate, you know? I know you see it," she said to the playful dog. Just then Rico came back in.

"I see you found the three stooges. They won't scare anyone," he said, making a statement that she was clearly on to the wrong dogs. "Well, correction, unless you count making someone laugh to death." She looked at him and they both had a smirk on their faces. "Want to pet them anyway? They are super cute!"

She motioned yes and in she went. They all rallied around her, knocking into each other for attention and into her legs. She grabbed the toy and threw it and two minutes later after amusing themselves and negotiating who got to hold it in their mouth and bring it back, they came back with the toy for another throw. She couldn't take her eyes off these ridiculous little creatures. They made her laugh

Sufani Weisman-Garza

and that was priceless. She needed laughter at this time in her life and with them it was effortless.

Rico watched outside the kennel and when she turned around, he was there to let her out. He opened the door for her and she stepped out. The dogs followed her to the door and all became silent, looking up at her as if to say, why are you leaving?

"OK," she said looking at Rico and then back into the kennel.

"Okay? What does that mean? You want this one?" and he pointed into the kennel at one of the bulldogs, confused.

"No," she said. "Not the one, I'll take them all."

Rico's eyebrows raised the highest they could go. "All?"

"Yes! I can't break up the band, clearly. They're hilarious! And I could use hilarious right now."

"Oh, I see." His eyebrows furrowed, nodding silently, and looking down. "Well, there is something you must know about them. They are a lot of work."

"So am I," she exclaimed.

He smiled. "You have to clean their wrinkles daily or they can get infections."

"Okay, I have endless time."

"They swallow air because it's hard for them to breathe, so they fart a lot."

She perked up her head away from looking at the dogs that were like statues looking at her. "So do I."

Sufani Weisman-Garza

Rico let out an immense laugh and she began to crack up to. The dogs began to jump around in a circle with each other almost celebrating their release.

"Okay," he said. "Let's do the paperwork and I'll give you more info on the dogs and their care. Because they're adults, they all have had some health issues, but they've been remedied here and they all have a great bill of health now. They came in separately. This one" and he pointed to the largest of them, "came in about three months ago. The other two just got here within a few weeks. So, they are all from different homes."

"Okay," was all she said. An hour later the paperwork was done, the list of ailments of their past and how to care for them was all ascertained and now for the walk home. She looked down at their short legs.

"They can walk, right? I mean, back to my house?"

Rico smiled at her. "Of course, your house was the one for sale, so I know where it is. It's not far. I think they can handle that. Just know they can't walk too long, or too far. Breathing becomes hard for them and they will literally just stop walking on you when they're tired. Here's my card," and he handed it to her. "If they poop out on you on the way home, call me and we'll send someone over to get you home, okay?"

She took the card. "Thank you."

At that, he handed her all the dogs on the leashes, and they all looked up at her eager to be led by her. Clearly,

74

they had had enough of the dog spa.

"Alright, let's hit it," she said to them, and they walked out the door to journey back to the house. The walk home was effortless, and they seemed very happy to be out and about with the fresh breeze on their faces. They walked a slow pace, but steady and followed her well looking up at her often trying to know her better. The steps up the house made them use more effort, but they all did it on their own. They stood on the porch looking up at her, anxious to go inside, as she put the key in the door and opened it. As soon as she opened the door to the house, she dropped their leashes, and they ran inside and played again, as if they were stoked that this was their new home. They romped about and ran into the long hallway and slid around on the hardwood floor and then came back to her when they were done. She had stayed where she was in front of the door just watching them and how adorable they were. They sat at her feet and rubbed against her and then individually they began to just look in different direction surveying the expanse of their new territory.

She unhooked their leashes and placed them on the table in the entry way. They stood up and wandered a bit, but stayed close and their bodies were so stocky they could hardly turn around.

"You guys are like walking table tops." She laughed to herself and how cute they were. "Let's go into the kitchen and I'll get you some water and then I am off to the store to go grocery shopping and I'll get you food and treats." They followed her and watched her create a space for their feeding. They each got a drink of water and then looked at her as she sat at the table watching them.

"Now for names. I know you are adults, but you deserve great fun names." The dogs were made up of two males and one female. All fixed, so there would be no breeding issues. All she needed was a bitch in the house that needed a caesarean section.

"Okay, you" and she pointed to one, and he came near her knees, "you will be called, 'Nos'; you're huge and it suits you best. You." She pointed to the girl and she waddled near on her front feet while looking directly at her. "You will be my little Ferrah." Ferrah waddled a little more and came closer and rubbed up against her leg and then looked at her endearingly. Jo gave her a scratch on the forehead and she sat at her side. "And you last." He looked at her, as though about to receive his medal of honor. "Your name, sport, will be, 'Tu'." He did not move. "Well, do you like it?" And at that he snorted his acceptance and began romping again with the group. "Together you are Nos-Ferrah-Tu, see?" They made no acknowledgement that they were named after a classic. They didn't seem to mind. They were happy to be where they were and with her and their friends. "I guess this makes you guys' brothers and sister now. I'm the mom, in case you wondered."

1377 Rikoppe Lane

They were funny dogs, always seeming to have the look of being lost and not knowing where to go, or what to do, but happily. She proceeded to show them around the house downstairs showing them the lie of the land and they seemed quite comfortable. Ferrah even jumped up on the couch in the library and began to take a nap. Tu joined Ferrah in the library and lay on the rug while Nos followed her around the house. She was in the kitchen making a list for groceries and Nos, loyal through and through, lay at her feet, occasionally looking up at her, as if to see if she needed anything. She just smiled at him. "God, you're cute as can be with your brown and white patch on your face." He revealed a tooth from his undershot jaw, a smile in his world she supposed, and it made her laugh and smile even more. She continued writing her list, not forgetting to get all the things the dogs needed to be happy and all the snacks she needed to be comforted.

She reached for her keys and purse, with shopping list in hand and was ready to leave to the market to get a few things. She had to go right away because the dogs needed food. So did she for that matter. She walked down the hallway lined with her bookshelves and a nice lamplit sofa table against the wall. Nos got up and walked with her. She looked down and he looked up. She smiled at him and he showed her his tooth. They walked to the library and saw Ferrah and Tu passed out in the same spot she left them in the library.

Sufani Weisman-Garza

"Okay, you guys, Mom is going to the store to get you num-nums and I will be back. No parties, no beer pong, or girls over while I'm gone."

Ferrah raised her head from her lazy position on the couch to look at her.

"That goes for you too. No sneaking boys into the house."

Ferrah laid her head back down, clearly having no plans that exciting.

Jo walked to door and Nos continued by her side and tried to walk out with her. When she stopped and looked down, he was looking up at her as if to say, "What?" He assumed he was going to the store with her.

"Oh, I see," Jo said. "You're the loyal one, the adult of the bunch, but always want to be with Mummy." He continued to stare at her and she smiled. She paused for a moment thinking. "Okay, you're going! Go get the leash." And she pointed to the chair in the entry. Surprisingly he went and got it and came back, leash in mouth. Surprised by his cleverness and ability to take orders, she soon began to wonder about other chores she could ask him to do and then laughed. "Okay, little man. I have no idea if dogs are allowed in the stores around here, but I don't care. I'm not going to even ask or look for signs. My father always told me that asking increased your chances of hearing a no, so I just don't ask, I do. Let's hit it." And she fastened his leash and they headed to the car and off to the store. The

78

other two were left happily sleeping like the dead in the library without a care in the world.

Sufani Weisman-Garza

Eleven

Returning home from the store, she slipped the old key in the lock, and it jammed. Holding two cloth bags in her left hand, the dog leash on her right wrist, and the key in the same hand, she muttered, "Oh great," and put down the bags. She took the key out of the lock and tried it again. Nos was confused but stood and watched her. She tried it again and still it would not budge. She dropped the leash from her wrist and began down the front steps drawn to look at the house for some reason. "Stay there, Nos," she said, pointing to him to stay on the large porch, as she went down the steps not knowing why. She went in front of the house and just looked at the front door and then up. The midday sun had crossed over the house and was shading the front side now as it approached later afternoon. There was nothing to see, but the house and the room with its almost blacked out windows above. No matter what time of day it was, it just never seemed to have any light shine through. It was strange, but nothing looked amiss, and she didn't even know why she felt drawn to do what she just did. Maybe to come at the door and lock with a fresh energy, who knew? She walked back up the steps and stood next to Nos and put the key in the door.

"Open, damn it!" When she twisted the key, it unlocked, and she exhaled a sigh of relief. "Oh, thank God," she said in one breath. Nos went in and looked around

80

cautiously and she grabbed the bags and went in and locked the door behind her. She passed the library, and the dogs were not where she left them. She thought for a moment, weren't dogs supposed to bark at the front door to people coming up to the door? All the dogs she had ever seen did that. Maybe her funny dogs were different.

She turned right and walked through the living room into the dining area, put her purse and keys on the table and then went into the kitchen and put her bags down. Nos followed her but had stopped in the dining room. With the bags on the counter, she began to unload them. She looked over to see that Nos had found the dogs under the dining room table, standing alert and looking at her. She walked over to the table and kneeled eye level with them.

"I got dinner," she said, but it did not immediately entice them out from under the table. Ferrah let out a whimper. "What's wrong with you guys? Come out! Momma's home and I got food, and wine." And she reached in the bag and pulled out the wine and bag of food to show them. She put the bag and wine down on the table and reached over to them and they both came waddling out from under the table to her arms and she gave them hugs, rubs, and kisses. After their hugs, the other two began to socialize with Nos. They seemed scared and it was strange, but perhaps it was being in a new house that was just unsettling to them. She put the groceries away and filled up the brand-new silver-colored bowls she bought for them, one each, and placed them on the floor in the corner of the dining room. They could all eat together when they did eat. It was a bit early for dinner, but she felt it was good to make them feel safe and at home. She went and began to put away all the other groceries and when done took out her salad spinner and began preparing a nice salad for the week to be placed in a stainless steel bowl, placing a paper towel below and above the lettuce preserving it all week long. The salad and greens from the market were so fresh and delicious and she ate pieces of the chopped vegetables as she prepared them. It was beginning to feel like home. After the salad was prepared, she fiddled around in the kitchen and then sat down at the marble island in the kitchen and wrote on a notepad meals that she would prepare for her sister and mother when they arrived. She got noticeably colder and got up from the table to look out the window in the kitchen and could see just the tip of the harbor water. It was getting darker outside, and the air was getting colder. She turned around from the window and all the dogs were at her feet in every direction around her but looking out and away from her. As she looked up to see what they were looking at a frightening sound rang out throughout the house.

It was a human sigh, and truly frightening being that no one was in the house but her. It was not a creak, or the house settling, this was the sound of a female voice, but it was everywhere in the house. Chills ran up her spine and the hair on the back of her neck and arms stood on end. The air became so cold that she could see her breath.

"What the fuck?" she yelled out in a panic, her breath materializing in the air. The dogs began growling, but at what? She ran to the back door with the dogs close behind running with her, their paws slipping on the floor, and she stood outside the house on the back porch landing with the door open and looking in down the hallway. It was lit with an amber light and she stood there for many minutes watching, as did the dogs, but nothing happened. Her breathing began to settle, and her heart rate slowed to a normal rate again the longer she stood there and nothing happened. She noticed that it was warmer on the porch than it had been in her house just before the noise. The dogs did not bark or growl, they simply stood at attention looking into the home in the exact same way that she did. The two back rooms had night lights and all she could see from the back porch landing was the hallway and the staircase leading upstairs to the next landing.

As she began to feel how silly it was that she was behaving this way and standing outside on her back porch, the dogs' heads all turned toward the staircase. They were looking at the top of the stairs, but there was nothing there. They growled and their eyes all began following something, as it lowered one step at a time down the stairs. Her eyes saw nothing. Their growls became more intense and then suddenly they whipped their necks over to the top right of the stairs landing like they saw something else enter. She didn't know what to do. She froze with the dogs, staring at nothing. They saw something, they all did. After a few more minutes on the porch, the dogs began to show signs of calm, no longer looking at the staircase, or anything in particular in the house and so she walked back inside cautiously. What else was she going to do, sleep on the porch? She had no idea what had just happened.

Nos, Ferrah, and Tu followed her reluctantly. She went into the kitchen, shaken and trembling, nervously looking around the house and took the cell phone out of her purse on the kitchen countertop. She punched in Doctor Donovan's number. She needed to talk to someone, she was scared. When he answered, she feverishly began telling him what had just happened and suddenly looked back at her purse remembering; hadn't she left it on the table in the dining room?

Twelve

When the doctor came in a few minutes after 8 am, she had already been in his office sitting and waiting patiently for him. Lucy had already let her in to his office. He came in one hour earlier than normal to squeeze in her unexpected visit. When he entered, briefcase and topcoat on his arm, he let out a tired morning sigh.

She tilted her head as if apologizing non-verbally. "Sorry, Doctor, to have you come in so early. You must think I am totally ridiculous." He shook his head no and smiled as he put his coat and bag on the top of his desk gracefully and quickly sat down in front of her on his chair. "Not at all, Johannah. Have you had time to think about the incident last night and come to any different conclusions?"

"Well, I didn't call the police as you recommended because there was literally nothing to report physically. The only physical thing I could pinpoint was the dogs' reaction to something. I took them with me around the house and then ultimately just tried to carry on like nothing. We went into the living room and watched TV and I probably went to my room much later than I would have and locked the door."

"Why is that?" he asked.

"Well, the dogs were looking at something coming down the stairs from the landing and then their necks whipped

85

to the right, like something else came in, and then all of the sudden it was like whatever they were watching got spooked and left. It was weird, Donovan." He looked at her and she corrected herself, "Oh, sorry, Doctor," she enunciated, drawing out the title. "I'm not much into formality." He didn't respond but kept the conversation moving.

"What do you think it was?" he asked.

"A freaking ghost! Haven't you watched *Paranormal Witness*?"

"Those movies are fake documentaries. You know that right?" he asked her, sure of himself.

"Those are the movies called *Paranormal Activity*. I'm talking about *Paranormal Witness*. That shit is scary!" And she looked at him with deeply bagged and darkened eyes with her head cocked to the right and almost humorous. There was a moment of silence and then they both burst out laughing. "Oh, that felt good," she said, exhaling from the laughter.

His body language relaxed. "You don't think that maybe," he said slowly, "that you are overreacting? A lot has been and is going on for your right now, and you are in mourning, and you live alone, and you weren't expecting that either at this time in your life. Do you think it is possible that some of your current experience is coming from a place of fear about your being alone, in a new state and new house?"

She thought about it and knew that it was an honest question, so she took her time with it. Rationally, she replied, "Yes, Doctor, I do think it definitely has something to do with it. I am scared in general right now, a feeling I am not used to. I needed to get away from my area, but in doing that and coming here I am dealing with the expected fears of being in a new place where everything is unknown. But I do feel like I am adjusting to the new place and people well. I am friendly and having friendly experiences with people, so I don't feel it is a negative. I feel that part of it is having normal fears that anyone would experience. Don't you think so?"

"Yes, it is very normal to have fears like that. Every person experiences those fears and anxieties in a move. You would be no different. It isn't a strength thing. It's just a change thing," he replied. She nodded, agreeing.

"I had a strange dream last night, too, when I went to bed," she said and leaned back into a very casual position on the chair, contemplating it in her head. "I was in my room. I mean, in the dream," she said looking over at him and then away again. "I went to sleep in my dream, in my room, and when I awoke in the dream I was in my bed, as I was in real life. A woman in Victorian period clothing, a white old-fashioned nightgown to be exact, was standing at the open door of my room. Across the way from my room is the other bedroom," she said looking at him explaining. "It is the room I have not touched yet. Anyway, the door to that room was also open across the darkened hall. The woman would not pass the doorway of my room. She stood in the doorway and looked at me. Her hair was in a loose style bun; an old hairstyle of the day and she pointed into the room across the hall that was completely black on the inside. You couldn't see anything." She paused. "You know, whenever I have looked into that room from the outside it is like that! It's just like blackness, no light whatsoever in there, which is strange. It has windows and although it is shaded by the tree's, even more than my window, there seems to be not a speck of light let in. It's weird. Like some optical illusion." She continued with her dream. "Anyway, she looked at me and she was quite serious. She pointed at the room and then with her arms still pointing to the room she turned to me and was saying something that I could barely hear. It was like she was a million miles away talking to me from space on a two-way radio. Like a faint radio connection that you could only hear pieces of the conversation too. She said three words over and over and I could hear the first word 'set' but couldn't make out the other two. She said over and over the three words desperately wanting me to understand what she was saying, knowing I couldn't make it out completely and then I woke suddenly from my dream. I was in a cold sweat, lying down and I looked at my door and it was closed and locked as it was when I went to bed. The dogs were silent on the bed in various places lying around me. All was quiet."

"And how did you feel when you woke up?" he asked.

Looking off into space she said, "I felt like I wish I could have heard what she was saying. It seemed important to her," she said and looked at him. "It felt like someone herding cats, impossible – frustrating!"

"Look, Jo. You're having a tough time right now. The last thing you need to do is to start focusing on being scared of your new house. When are your mother and sister coming?"

"My sister is coming tomorrow and my mother on Thursday," she informed him.

"Okay. What I want you to do is stay focused on what needs to be done to prepare for your sister. Do you have things that need to be done to get ready for her?"

"Yes, I need to get items from the store and make her room ready. I know specific snack foods she likes and things she needs in her bathroom that she always seems to forget from her travel case. And I was planning on having her help me decorate the room across from mine, the room in the dream. I thought it could be a good project," she said and looked at him for his thoughts.

"Yes, great idea. Get things that your sister needs in the house for her arrival. If you have left over time today, perhaps get things for the room you'll need, paint or whatever," he said looking at her and shaking his head for understanding. "Then, for the evening make yourself a nice meal and maybe rent a movie that has always made you feel good or laugh. Create comfort around you that feels familiar," he said, reassuring her.

"I see," she said nodding. "Things that have always made me feel good in the past or feel regular."

"Right! You need to be focused on good things right now. I think you took a good step in the right direction by going to the farmers' market the other day and getting your dogs. It says that you're putting down roots and getting to know your neighbors. Give yourself some breathing time, Jo. It takes time to settle into a home and a town. Having some family around will do you good and make you feel better. You'll see." And he smiled at her, folding his hands together. Her time was up.

She looked at the clock. "OK. Time's up! Well, you gave me some good things to be focused on. I think I'll leave here and go to Mamma's for some breakfast, but stop at home to get the dogs first." And she smiled and looked at him and then stood. He stood as she did. "Thank you, Doctor." And she smiled at him, and he returned the gentle smile. "See you in a few days for my real appointment."

"Yep, I have you in the schedule," he said confirming and opened the door for her to exit the room. He did not come out of the room but simply waved her goodbye and left the door open as he went in and disappeared into the room.

"Thank you, Lucy," she said in a soft voice as she left

the office. Lucy was on the phone but looked up and managed to wave and smile at her on the way out. Getting into her car she pulled out a paper from her purse and made a list of things she needed to get done before Layce arrived. The list grew long, and she knew she had a good long day of activity planned, enough to keep her busy. She knew exactly what movie she would watch too, *When Harry Met Sally*. She always loved that movie. She kept her mind on the busyness she planned for herself during the day, conveniently putting off the anxiety of the night-time that would come; the night-time that frightened her now in that old house.

Thirteen

After an uneventful night in the house, she woke up with the dogs on her bed. Tu and Ferrah were at her feet while Nos lay beside her. He clearly was the alpha male and she, his claimed prize. When the other two got distracted, Nos always stayed by her side and was eager to go out with her anywhere she would go when the other two would choose lounging in the warmth of the house. She had a special affection for Nos and his loyalty, although loved the other two dearly. She had been so busy with getting herself and the house ready for her sister and watching funny movies the night before that she had almost forgotten her fear in the house completely. She and the dogs enjoyed themselves and she felt the doctor had really helped her talk it through. She knew it could not have been her imagination completely because the dogs sensed something and were seeing something, but whatever that moment was, it had not repeated itself last night. She lay in bed for a few moments and her mind went to Clay. She felt a pain in her spirit seeping out from the space in her heart she had locked up. She had carefully concealed that part of her until she could deal with all of it. Perhaps little doses were her way of grieving. Perhaps it was her way of not wanting to let Clay go so fast. If she held on to him and let go of only small pieces at a time, he would stay with her longer. But already life was moving on and change was

92

happening. Her sadness for his loss was coupled with a deep sorrow of being abandoned. She supposed that at some point it would be prudent to talk about it with the doctor. It would be healthy to talk about what she was feeling. She began to stir and stretch in bed, bumping the dogs who seemed irritated by being asked with a nudge to move. "Time to get up, midgets," she said to her bulldogs. Tu looked at her funny. "I know it's not politically correct," she said staring at him. "But you're not really a little person, so it's funny. I can call you a midget because you're a dog!" He tired of her conversation and turned his head and placed his chin back on his paw. "Whatever, Tu. Ferrah, let's get up now and get ready for Layce. She's my sister," she said explaining to her. "You guys are gonna love her."

She jumped off the bed and got in the shower. While washing, she remembered the dream she had. The same woman in white, at the door, saying something, "Set (inaudible), (inaudible)." What was she saying? Her voice was a million miles away in the dream. Still, she pointed into the darkness of the room across from hers as she stood in the doorway looking at her, telling her something important. The dream didn't feel like just a dream. Dreams were forgotten so quickly, but this, she still remembered. She soon went on about her business and got dressed for the day and went downstairs, fed the dogs and herself and headed out the door to get Layce. It was Tuesday morning, a crisp day, clear outside, and she was excited to pick up her sister and show her around town, her new house, and her dogs. While in the kitchen, she informed the dogs while they ate that they would stay at home while she was getting her sister at Tacoma Narrows Airport.

"I'll be back shortly with a new member of the family for you to meet." She took them out for a bathroom run in the back yard before leaving and then brought them back inside. "Now you guys hang out in the living room, or library, or something and relax. I'll be back real soon. Love you guys." And she grabbed her purse and keys and headed to the front door. Nos followed her and looked up at her as if he was going too. She knelt down next to him.

"Nos, I can't take you this time just in case I have to go into the airport or something. I don't believe in leaving dogs in cars and I don't want to be potentially faced with that decision, okay?" and she scratched his ears and the side of his face with both hands. He seemed to be okay with it and walked back to join the others in the library.

As Jo pulled up to the pickup curb, Layce was already there. She instantly noticed her car ten feet away and began jumping up and down in excitement. Layce never cared who was looking. She was pure joy and had no shame in expressing herself that way. It was her best feature. Johannah pulled up to the curb and got out. Layce walked to meet her at the curb and gave her a big hug. She had a blonde Marilyn Monroe hairdo with chestnut lowlights and colorful barrettes holding her hair back on one side. She was stylish in a comfortable way and always wore lots of color. Perhaps her having to be in black all the time at the spa made her do the exact opposite in her civilian clothes. They hugged and squeezed one another for a good twenty seconds before letting go. Layce held her shoulders and moved her back away just a bit to look at her sister.

"You look amazing!"

Jo smiled. "Thanks, Sis. You hungry?"

"Starved," Layce replied.

"OK, let's go get some breakfast. I found this really cute cafe near my house called Mamma's, we'll go there."

Luggage was promptly put in the car and off they went back to Gig Harbor. Jo drove thinking how good it felt to have family around. She was ready for interaction now, even questions. Even questions at high velocity, which was generally the only way Layce asked them. She smiled to herself. She felt happy. Being with family had made her feel happy again and to her that was a sign that she must be in recovery and turning a corner in her life. She drove with Layce while smiling from ear to ear, as they caught up and drove to the cafe. This felt right.

Sufani Weisman-Garza

Fourteen

Pulling into the driveway of Mamma's Cafe, Jo realized how hungry she was. It was still early enough to get breakfast. "You hungry, baby sister?" Jo asked.

"Famished! This is cute," Layce said, looking around at the surroundings.

Jo shut off the car and they both got out after grabbing their purses. Layce wrapped her left arm around Jo's right and walked close with her chatting all the while they walked to the door. It would be clear to any onlookers that they were sisters. Sisters just had a way of creating an energy that said home.

Jo opened the door to Mamma's Cafe and let Layce in first.

"Well, hello, stranger," came a voice as they walked in.

Jo looked around to the right and realized it was coming from Ginni, the funny barista she had met before.

"Oh, hey, Ginni! Good to see you." Quickly she ushered Layce over to introduce her to Ginni who was again behind the counter making a drink. "This is my sister, Layce. Layce, this is Ginni. She's my new friend in Gig Harbor." She looked at Ginni and winked. "Her boyfriend helped me find my dogs!"

Ginni smiled.

"*You got dogs?*" Layce asked, excitedly. In all the

96

excitement, Jo had forgotten to tell Layce she adopted her rather unthreatening group of misfit-huffers.

"Oh, yes! I totally forgot to tell you."

Ginni cut in, "Are you guys here for breakfast?"

"Yes, that's why we came, actually," Jo said cheerfully.

Ginni smiled. "Go ahead and pick a seat," she said pointing to the other side of the cafe that had booths for more dining experiences, "and someone will be with you. Jo, your yoozh?"

"Tall, double, soy cap!" Jo repeated.

"Yep, that's how I remember it," Ginni said. "Layce, what's your drink?" And she looked her dead in the face.

"Oh," she said surprised by the hospitality and directness. "Short, triple shot café mocha! Put hair on my chest, Ginni. Let's see whatcha got!" Layce was playful and made friends easily with her ability to adapt with people and make them feel like she'd known them forever. They were instant friends,

Ginni was the same way. Perhaps that was why Jo liked her too. "You got it, Layce. I'll personally deliver these to make sure it's hairy enough." And she winked at Layce, then smiled at Jo and walked back behind the bar. "Sit anywhere," she yelled out as her back was to them and she pointed them into the dining room. "We're informal here."

They both smiled and looked at each other and surveyed their pickings. They settled on a table by the front window to look out. Layce wanted to look more at the area too.

"I like it already, Sis. It's friendly here. You needed this place. Ginni's cute!" she said with a big smile and looking at Jo. "Your intuition was right to pick this place." Jo's face must have shown some doubt for a split second because Layce picked up on it. Nothing got by Layce. "You do like it, don't you?"

"Oh, God, yes! I love it," Jo replied.

"Then what was that look? I saw it. It was only there for a second, but something came into your mind when I said it. What is it?"

"It's nothing." She was quiet for a moment and looking down at the table they had seated themselves at. "Well, it's the house. I guess," she said, a little confused and slightly uncomfortable.

Layce remained quiet for a moment studying Jo's face but was unable to place the facial expression. "Hey," she said softly, and reached out for her hand on the table. "What's going on, Sis? You can tell me."

Just then the young waitress came and said hello, then gave them menus to look over. They did and promptly ordered their food and then continued.

"I *love* the house. It's amazing. But I've been having weird dreams and a few weird things have happened in the house."

"Weird, like how?" Layce asked, concerned, with brow furrowed.

Jo didn't want to say too much to Layce. She needed her to remain unbiased and hadn't planned on telling her anything, but Layce had a way of getting a person to tell everything instead.

Jo simply said, "Just lots of noises in the house, that sort of thing."

"Is that all?" Layce complained. "Sister, it's an old Victorian. You better get used to a lot of noises from an old Victorian. Don't worry; I'll be there with you now for a while, so you have me to protect you." Layce smiled facetiously.

Jo laughed out loud.

"What? I can protect you," Layce said, trying to be convincing.

"You can't even protect me from spiders, Layce," Jo said playfully.

"Oh, shush. You know I can too. I'm sweet but I could kick some ass if I needed too. You aren't the only one who stayed in West Covina for a few years. We learned some street savvy there and had our share of fights in the neighborhood. If I needed to protect you, I could, so don't dismiss me so quickly," she said, slightly tipping her head enough to mean business.

"You should snap your finger in the air after you say that," Jo said, laughing at her sass. "I know you have a tough side, just like me."

"Let's hurry up and eat and get home. I'm dying to

see this house and those protection dogs. Okay, tell me all about them."

Just as she said that Ginni came walking toward them and Layce looked up at her, so Jo turned around to see what she was looking at. Ginni put Jo's drink down first knowing it would satisfy.

"OK, what do you think?" Ginni said handing the mocha to Layce.

Layce took it from her and looked at her, squinting her eyes and puckered her lips skeptically. She took a sip and Ginni cocked her head to the right, looking at her face for a reaction. Layce put it down on the table, not yet showing her cards.

"Ooh, very good!" she said in her animated over-the-top style. "Strong with still a hint of sweetness. Some people don't put the right amount of chocolate; either too much, or not enough."

"Yah, you looked like you would like the coffee taste, but you seem like a person with a sweet tooth. They tell you to put four pumps of mocha, but for you I did three. Four would have taken over the coffee. So, is this a winner? If so, I will commit it to memory. I like remembering people's drinks. It says a lot about people."

Layce smiled at her, nodding a yes.

"Oh, and what does my drink say about me?" Jo asked.

"A cappuccino drinker? Okay," she said playing along.

"Notoriously picky; likes things how they like it; kind, but precise; not afraid of change and feel they should get what they paid for straight up. If they didn't, they have no qualms about politely insisting it be done until accurate."

Layce and Jo both burst out into laughter and even Ginni was amused.

"Boy, did you nail it. That's exactly you, Jo," Layce said.

"I've been coffee scoped." Jo chuckled.

"Gotta get back to work," Ginni said, unfazed by her accuracy. "Layce, you make sure you come back in now."

"Oh, I will, for sure. I like to run in the morning, so maybe on the way back toward the house I'll stop in for coffee. You'll be here tomorrow morning?"

"Yep, every morning at 8 am."

"Perfect. See you soon, then."

Ginni shot her with an invisible hand gun in her right hand, as she walked away winking at her.

Jo and Layce ate their breakfast joyfully and then headed to the house. Jo knew Layce would be amazed at the sheer size and beauty of the house and couldn't wait to show her, as well as introduce her to Nos-Ferrah-Tu.

Fifteen

On the car ride home, they were smiling, but also somewhat quiet, the type of quiet that comes over you when you are at peace with another person. Layce was looking around at the beauty, the harbor, the birds, and the trees everywhere, old and bordering the streets. She cracked the window and brought her nose to it for a moment to smell the fresh harbor air. It was indeed a beautiful setting and the windy road leading to her house made the landscape that much more magical. They were getting closer to the house when Jo commented, "You know Ginni has a boyfriend?"

Layce smiled at her coyly. "You know, Jo, just because a bisexual woman is friendly with another woman doesn't mean she wants to date her; but she is hot!" she said smiling at her sister. "I'm not here for anything else, but to hang out with my sister. But you know how friendly I am. People like me! I can't help it; I make friends easy. Besides, she was as friendly to me as I was to her. It was effortless, actually," she said looking down, picking lint off her skirt.

"Yah, it did seem to flow very easy. She is an extrovertish person too, I think," Jo assessed. "Even when I met her, it kind of flowed, but she had more sparkle with you than me for sure." Jo looked at her and smiled.

"You have to be sparkle to get sparkle, Jo, dear sister!" And she batted her eyes at her playfully, as they pulled into the driveway. Jo saw her eyes go directly up to the windows above to 'the room'. "Wow, this is it, huh?" She fell silent and in awe like she was taking it all in with caution. "Wow."

Jo just looked at her, watching her look around the house.

"Man! And you can see the harbor and everything from here. And there's a wraparound porch? How cool is that?" She got out of the car and started walking toward the house looking up at the window above the porch.

"Hey!" Jo called out.

Layce turned around.

"Bags?"

"Oh. Oh ya. Hehe. Sorry." Layce ran back to the car, got her bag and they went up the stairs to the porch. The dogs were barking at the front door, knowing Jo had returned.

"Well, get ready to meet my pack of misfits. They couldn't protect you," she said taking out her old key from her purse, "but they could make someone laugh to death."

Layce grabbed her hand with the key before she put it in the door. "Wow, look at that key!"

"Yah, I know, as old as the house. Cool, huh?"

Layce only shook her head in amazement and then looked at the door.

"Be careful, they are clumsy and stocky. They're like walking tabletops and turn before they look, so they can knock you over. They're a great bunch, though," she said, turning the key and opening the door.

Out they came onto the porch, accosting her with love and licks. Ferrah tried to jump on Layce only making it to above her ankle. Layce promptly let down her bags and played with the dogs who immediately loved her. Mostly Ferrah, who continued to stay close to her and looked into her eyes as often as she could. Nos continued to be loyal as the day was long to Jo and never left her side. Tu was quickly becoming the neutral party, the mediator. Slow and steady.

As Layce looked up at the house in the foyer, the hallway lengthened, the house was luxurious beyond what she had imagined in the most ancient and elegant of ways. It was an understated elegance kissed by time. It was looking at a time gone by yet happily living in the present. "Wow, Jo! This is something!" she said, looking at the ceiling, the rooms, the furniture, and carpets. She was clearly in a state of awe and needed a moment to take it all in. The dogs also got quiet, watching her every move.

Sixteen

Jo watched as her sister looked around the place with awe. She walked from room to room downstairs making her way to the end of the house and finding her way to the back entrance staircase. She held the banister and placed one foot on the first step and then down again. All the while looking up. She looked over at Jo who had been following her from room to room.

"This is it!" Layce exclaimed. She looked at Jo and then up the staircase again almost hesitantly. "May I go up?"

"Oh! Sure," Jo said, taking the lead to be the host, as though she had forgotten her manners. "It is my house, so I suppose I should show you around. Why did you take your foot off the step? Just curious," she said as Layce looked at her.

"I don't know. I got a sort of silent feeling inside," she said explaining no more.

Jo didn't ask her what she meant. Layce had always had her own way of explaining things and she sort of always just knew what Layce meant. She had also had that feeling in the home the first time and remembered herself not even entering the second floor until the second day in the house. It just had something that made you stop and take it all in; at least that's what she felt in her first moment with the house.

As Layce began to ascend the stairs with Jo, Jo went

back down to the front door to get the bags. When Jo came to the back staircase, Layce had already made it up the stairs and was not in sight. Jo climbed up the stairs with her luggage and found Layce in front of the third bedroom door, the room she did not usually go in, the cold room.

"What are you doing?"

"What's in there?" Layce asked. Her mood was cautious, as she whispered.

"Uh, a bedroom, goofy. What else?" Jo returned facetiously. "This is your room, though." And she pointed to the room before hers that was joined by a wall to her room. She opened the door to the room in which Layce would be staying and Layce abandoned the door of the cold room, having never seen it yet, to take a look at her room.

"Ooh, this is lovely. Wow, look at the wallpaper," she said touching the velvet. "Look at this bathtub," as she walked into the large bathroom. Walking back out, she commented, "Sis, you did a really nice job keeping it a period piece. Look how all the furniture fits with the time period. I mean, at least it looks like it. I don't really know of course. But wow, you did a great job."

Jo smiled. "Thanks, Sis. It kept me busy. Want to see my room?" Her eyebrows lifted and Layce excitedly shook her head in yes. As they walked to her room, she opened the door and Layce briefly looked at the door to the room across from Jo's and then into Jo's room. As Layce looked around at all her things, she smiled and touched her items and Jo began to talk about their schedule.

"I have a doctor's appointment tomorrow, but was thinking that the next few days, starting tomorrow after my appointment; we can work on the room across from mine. It's the only one I haven't touched yet. I was waiting for you."

"Oh, yah? Why? There's something…creepy about it, huh, Sis?" And she looked in the room's general direction. She was serious.

"*What*? You haven't even seen it yet. How would you know that?" Jo said, playing off that she hadn't hit the nail on the head. Layce was empathic and intuitive. She felt things in her being perhaps a little more than Jo did.

They both sat on Jo's bed and faced each other. It was something that sisters did. They were old friends and knew when to sit and have a quick chat. It was an unspoken thing they did even as kids.

"There is something," Jo said and then her voice fell away.

"Yah, something," Layce said, confirming, looking over at the door from Jo's bed. "But we'll investigate it further tomorrow. Right now, it should be about fun. Help me unpack and then maybe we can watch a movie, or go get some yogurt or, I don't know, take a walk? Just something normal! How's that sound?"

"Sounds great," Jo said and smiled a soft and sweet

Sufani Weisman-Garza

smile.

"Plus, I want to play with those dogs. Where are they, anyway?" she said, looking around.

"Oh, I think they stayed downstairs. Sometimes it's too much work for them to come up the stairs, so they just wait for me downstairs. They do come up to sleep with me, though. They're bed hogs for sure."

"Can Ferrah sleep with me tonight?" she said smiling and bouncing up and down on the bed like she was a little girl.

"If she wants to. It's free will in this house. I think she will want to, though. She seemed to really take to you."

"I know! She's a cutie pie."

"Let's get you unpacked and then hang out a bit. Maybe we'll take the dogs for a walk, and I can show you the neighborhood and where the farmers' market is. Stuff like that."

"OK, sounds great!" Layce said and they walked back to Layce's room and began to settle her in.

The dogs waited patiently in the library for their return to the first floor.

Seventeen

Layce and Jo had walked around town and picked up some snacks and assorted items that Layce liked, as well as something to make for dinner. Layce wasn't a meat eater; fish was okay, on occasion, but she lived as a vegetarian, although she wasn't into the labels. Jo picked up some tofu and other organic items to make dinner for Layce and her mother when her mother arrived. They returned home and made an easy dinner – potato and eggs, just like their mother used to make. It was hot, fast, and just plain tasted good. Neither of them was up to making a full formal dinner. Traveling always put a strain on one's energy and even preparing for guests, although welcome, is also a strain. They simply wanted to settle in and take it easy. Tomorrow was another day.

It was now dark outside, and they had been sitting and watching TV and playing with the dogs for a while. Playing was an exaggeration. Playing involved a tickle on their neck or stomach and them licking you, or snorting. They were content being lazy on the couch and getting love. And who could blame them?

"Jo, I think I'm gonna go take a bath and get into my jammies. Want to watch *Casablanca* when I'm done?"

"Sure," Jo said smiling, remembering how they used to watch old movies together all the time. "Like old times! Maybe Mae West and Jean Harlow movies too some other time," she said looking to Layce for approval.

Layce simply smiled and nodded.

"Do you need help with anything upstairs, or are you good?"

"Oh, I'm good, Sis. You don't need to take care of me. I'm here for you," she said smiling at her sister and kissing her on the cheek, as she got up from the couch they were sitting on. "But I am gonna get some wine and listen to some music. Classical, on my phone. Gotta love Pandora music streaming," she said and smiled at her sister as she went into the kitchen, opened the fridge, poured a glass of Malbec, and headed up the back staircase to her room.

After another thirty minutes or so downstairs, Jo decided to go upstairs herself and change into her jams and wash off her make-up. Her sweet and clumsy pack of stooges followed her up the stairs, struggling to get their stocky bodies and little legs up each step. Nos was a fighter and Ferrah had lots of energy, but Tu just plain gave up three quarters of the way there and sat on the step, as though he had come to grips that it was where he would be the rest of the night. The other dogs looked back at him with subtle encouragement, as she did.

"Tu, that's all you got? You ran out of juice?" She headed back toward him and picked him up and put him on the landing. From there, she took the lead of the pack and they all walked behind her and into her room. She proceeded to change from her clothes into her bed clothes, wash her face and comb her hair, as the dogs lay on her bed watching her intently, fascinated with their mistress.

Layce had run the water nice and hot. The bathroom was wet with steam and the mirror was cloudy, the soft sound of her phone playing classical music was on the toilet seat and she lay in the bathtub with bubbles and a glass of wine, a happy woman. She felt at home there and felt like being there made things better for her sister who was experiencing pain she could not begin to know, having never been in a long-term relationship more than eight months, nor having lost a love, especially the way her sister lost Clay. She couldn't know her pain, but she could be there for her sister. She and Jo had a relationship that was such that they could be away from one another for a long while and when they were together again would feel as though not a day had passed. It was an amazing closeness they shared as sisters. The heat was slowly sedating her, and the music played in the background ever so softly. Steam rose from the still water she lay in; the water was very hot. The bathroom mirror beaded with condensation and dripped down, streaking the mirror from the steam. She took a sip of her wine leaving only a few more left. She could feel the wine do its job of relaxing her mind while the hot water relaxed her muscles that were often very sore from her line of work. Although she could not name modern classical artists, she had a fondness for the music. It brought her peace and calm. She had been lying in the water for some time and knew that soon she would need to get out. She consigned herself to getting out of the tub when the last drop of Malbec was drunk. She felt her head get cloudy from the steam and heat. It seemed to get hotter in the room, but it was just from the build-up of steam in the bathroom she had been in for over twenty, if not thirty, minutes. Her fingers were shriveled like prunes. Her head remained reclined, the music continued to play and the steam rise. The only sound was the sound of the sweet classical music that began to break slightly in and out with static. She looked over at her phone, thinking that Pandora must have a weak satellite signal. Turning her head back to a forward position and reclining her neck back again the music continued to come in and out of static until the static got stronger. But it was strange, the quality of the music was not interrupted, it was as if two sounds were playing at the same time and the static got louder and louder. Beginning to get annoyed, but with head still reclined back, she began to hear strange sounds in the static that sounded almost like whispers, or someone talking. Not just one voice but it sounded like several talking in rapid succession, but still it was in the static. The steam in the bathroom became unnaturally thick and she stirred, feeling something was off, something that brought her sixth sense to alertness. She opened her eyes to see the steam and her eyebrows creased in confusion. The static became clear. "Go under. Go under," she heard being whispered. Freaked out, she yelled for Jo and grabbed the side of the tub to climb out and saw a black figure of a little girl holding a doll begin to come forward and just then from the tile in the wall above and behind her, a phantom shadowy head emerged of a woman up to her bust in a white collard dress and black brooch, who screamed at the oncoming girl figure, the most unholy scream, as her face contorted toward the child. She was caught between some paranormal battle. Terrorized into silence, Layce flung her arms, water splashed, and the wine glass flew as she climbed out of the tub, grabbed her phone still streaming music and ran out of the bathroom, toward Jo's room, soaking wet and naked. The same unholy scream had chased her down the hall and she slammed the door shut to Jo's room when she entered. She was hysterical and her eyes were as big as silver dollars.

Eighteen

Jo jerked her head toward the door at Layce, shocked by her abrupt entrance. She stood up from her bed in her pajamas and the dogs got up on their feet when she came in.

"What the hell? Layce!" Jo said, going to her at once. Noticing her nakedness, she grabbed her a towel from the bathroom and a bed shirt. Layce grabbed the towel and locked the door to Jo's room. "What happened?" Jo said compassionately, ushering her sister to sit on the bed. When she led her, she noticed that there was blood. "Oh, my God, you're bleeding," she said and bent down to inspect her leg at once. In Layce's terror, she stepped on the broken glass from the wine glass that had fallen and made several deep cuts in her foot. Jo was careful not to touch the blood and took a moment to assess what she needed to do. She covered her cheeks with her hands for a moment. "Layce, this is bad," she said and looked up at her scared sister. "But it's gonna be okay," she said correcting her tone to reassure her. "Just take a deep breath, dry off and put on that shirt." Layce did what she said, as Jo went into her bathroom and got first aid supplies. As Layce's cuts were being tended too, she began to settle her breathing down.

"Seriously, what the hell is up with this house?" Layce demanded.

114

"What happened to you? Tell me now," Jo said.

"I was having a great time. It was peaceful. Then the air got thick and the steam got ridiculous. Sis, like ridiculous! Like someone just blew in more steam from somewhere. It gets less steamy as the heat of the water dies down, not *steamier*. I started hearing talking in the static of my music and then when I turned around to look there was a fucking shadowy little girl holding a dangly doll, and this thing came out from the tile and screamed at it. It was a woman. Her fucking face turned into the face from *Scream* the movie. I'm not joking! What is going on with this place?" She stared at Jo who was first and foremost focused on her sister's wounds before she could react or engage with anything other than needing to fix the cuts.

"You don't need stitches. You're lucky, sister." She wrapped up the third wound and then gave her sister socks to wear, mostly to protect the dressings. Jo stood up and took a deep breath. The dogs had since cuddled around Layce and she was calmed by the motion of petting them.

"Layce, honestly, I don't know. There is something happening here." And she began to fill Layce in on the smoking man shadow in the living room from her first night, the incident with something coming down the stairs that only the dogs could see, and something scaring it off, and her purse and keys that were moved mysteriously.

Layce was spooked and speechless. Jo was simply

too tired to be terrified, she had been through too much. She kept her head.

"We need to go back into the room to clean up the mess and the blood."

"I'm never taking a fucking bath in that room again," Layce stated emphatically.

Jo smirked. "No one is asking you too, Sis. From now on I will be in there with you when you take a bath, or shower, okay?" Layce nodded her head in agreement as they walked down the hall. They both paused after a few steps.

"Where's the water," Jo asked. There should have been not only water, but blood on the hallway floor. They moved forward and turned into the room. The fireplace was on, the room was cozy, and the bathroom door was open.

Layce grabbed Jo's pajama shirt and leaned close on her back behind her. "I didn't turn that on," she stated firmly referring to the fireplace. They both walked in together, scared of what they may find in the bathroom. To their surprise, the bathroom looked as if no bath had ever taken place, no wine glass was broken on the floor, no steam or steamed windows, no heat left by a recent bath, only dry floors, dry towels, and the bathroom was pristine, as though the incident never happened. Jo looked at the floor and walls and all around, then at Layce.

"I took a bath, sister," Layce said emphatically holding

her position of what had just happened.

"I know," Jo assured her. "Don't worry. Strange things happen in this house," she said moving backwards out of the bathroom with Layce at her back. Layce looked over her shoulder, not trusting anything.

"Where's the glass?" Jo asked rhetorically. There was no broken wine glass. And if it wasn't broken, where would a used wine glass be?

They both answered, "Downstairs," and they skidded down the hallway, down the back stairs to the kitchen. There by the sink sat a wine glass, having had no wine poured in it and sparkling clean. They both stood staring in disbelief, frozen for at least thirty seconds, not knowing what to do, think or understanding what was happening.

"Jo, I don't understand."

They walked around the counter into the dining room staring at the sink area and the lone wine glass and then sat at the table facing each other. They both looked down at Layce's foot that was wrapped in bandages.

"I have to look, Layce."

Layce was just as curious as she was. If there was no broken glass, how could her foot be cut?

Jo looked up and Layce gave her the nod of silent approval. They had to look at her foot. Layce lifted her foot to Jo's lap. Jo rested her calf sideways on her thigh and she began to unravel the cut that had been the deepest. After multiple rounds of unwrapping, the foot was exposed.

Sufani Weisman-Garza

"Jo, you saw the blood. You wrapped it for Pete's sake!"

Jo shook her head. "I did, Layce. I don't understand this." She continued to unwrap the two other bandages, and each was like the one before. There was nothing there but her bare foot and not a drop of blood on the cotton wrapping. They both looked for an extended amount of time at her foot in disbelief. Not a wound to be found.

"What about the trash in your bathroom? You wiped up the blood on the floor," Layce explained.

"No need to bother looking," Jo said looking up at her. "We both know it won't be there either."

They both sat there for a few minutes as the sounds of the dogs making their way down the stairs gave them a distraction they absolutely needed. Jo threw away the gauze wrapping in the kitchen sink trash and the dogs clamored around her legs. There was a glass candy dish in the kitchen filled with dog jerky. She took three bits out and gave each one of the dogs a treat.

"Well, let's go relax in the living room and do something normal like watch Casablanca. I'll make popcorn."

Layce looked up and sighed in agreement.

Jo looked at her after she put the popcorn in the microwave. "Want a glass of wine?" she said sarcastically.

"Fuck you," Layce said to Jo laughing, and Jo joined her in laughter as they walked past the dining room and

118

1377 Rikoppe Lane

into the living room, the three stooges in tow.

Sufani Weisman-Garza

Nineteen

She sat in the chair waiting for the doctor's reaction to the story she just told him of the night before. He was speechless. They just looked at each other.

"Look, Doc, I think this will probably be the last time I'm here in this capacity, as your patient."

He looked at her, surprised.

"Clearly, I have other things to deal with and with my family being here, well, they are my therapy, always have been."

He nodded his understanding, if not his approval.

"I know that the story I just told you sounds nuts but, honestly, I could use you more as a friend than a professional." She looked up at him and said, "Don't answer anything to that comment. It was rhetorical. I've just never been one to really seek therapy, although I value it." She reassured him. "I know I am not crazy because it would have had to be a dual delusion which isn't possible. Something weird happened in that house last night and has been happening to me since I got there. Remember my smoking shadow man the first night I slept in the living room?"

His eyebrows ascended and he said, "Oh, yes, I do remember."

"Look, you have lived here for some time, right?" she asked.

Sufani Weisman-Garza

"Yes, born here."

"Well, do you know anything about the house? Have there been any strange things happening in the house before I bought it, or anything that seemed strange with the tenants?"

"No. The house was owned by one family my whole life until recently when the old couple passed away, one after the other – not in the house," he made sure to explain. "The children sold the place having no need for it, and I believe they all moved out of the state somewhere else. I wasn't close with their children; nothing strange about them that I remember. A brother and sister, and they seemed like they had a normal childhood. You know, they seemed like every other family growing up. Beyond my life span, I don't know. You know that house was built in the eighteen hundreds?"

"Yes, I did know that, eighteen-ninety. I think I will do some historical research of the house and go to the Gig Harbor Historical Society to find out more about it," she said chin in hand, head lowered, thinking.

"Are you going to feel okay in the house?"

"Ah, well, I don't scare easily and it is my house," she said, stubbornly. "I'm more interested in finishing my work on the house and finding out what I can about it. It may lead to some answers."

"Question," the doctor asked. "Do you think you may be using this situation to avoid your grief and talking about it?"

She looked up surprised. "Ah, *no!*" she said, matter of fact. "If I started doing ghost-hunting in my home and buying ghost buster tools to dig stuff up, I would say I was distracting myself. But I can't help how my dogs are reacting, shadow figures appearing, or strange children holding floppy dolls and full-on heads screaming and coming out of tiles, or blood from fake cuts. It's here! I have to deal with it because it's in my face. I didn't go looking for this."

The doctor nodded his head, understanding her point, yet not knowing what to say about the occurrence she felt she was experiencing. His field was psychology, not paranormal activity. "Good. You've thought it through, and this is a reasonable statement. Do you feel however that you still need to talk about Clay?"

Her voice softened; her shoulders dropped. "I will, doctor, when I feel I want to have an outer conversation. I talk about Clay daily in my mind and honestly it is that conversation that makes me tired. I need a break from it. When I feel I need to talk, I assure you I will talk with my sister about it, or my mother. They are great listeners. Good people!" And she smiled. "You might see us all out at the farmers' market sometime."

He smiled and stood. "OK, then," he said. "Well, it was wonderful meeting you and I hope to see you out and about." And he held out his hand to shake and she took it.

"Doctor," she said, looking him in the eyes as they stood a foot apart. "You were the first person I made friends with since coming to this place, and I am very grateful to have met you and that I had you to talk to. You really gave me a sense of connection to a new place and had great advice that made me feel more like Gig Harbor is my home now."

He looked at her, smiled and released her hand.

"I do hope we can remain friends, as people, now that I am not a patient. Thank you for being here for me when I needed someone. It was great that it was you," and she reached out and hugged him.

He was clearly not used to getting hugged by patients and with a delayed embrace gave her a squeeze, slightly uncomfortable, as they separated.

"Yes, well, I am sure we will see each other around town. Take care," he said stepping back politely and smiling at her genuinely.

She grabbed her purse and left his office. As she walked to her car, she googled the historical society location and drove straight there from her appointment, before returning home. She had to know more about her house. Something had happened there; she just knew it. A strong wind blew, and she drove in the same direction to find out about her haunted house.

Sufani Weisman-Garza

Twenty

Since Jo was at her psych appointment, Layce decided she would jog over to Mamma's Coffee Shop to see Ginni, the funny (and cute) barista. She had told her she would stop by in the morning anyway and she didn't like to say things to people she didn't follow through on. Since her foot really wasn't bloodied and torn up, she could still jog. Plus, she needed coffee, and she wanted a coffee cake muffin if they had it, so it was a good excuse to go in. The dogs looked at her longingly to go with her as she approached the back door, but being that they had tiny legs, were built like tabletops and weren't very good at even walking, running was out of the question.

"Sorry, dudes and dudette, but auntie is going out on her own. I'll take you out for a walk when I get back, okay?" she said and bent down to give them last minute scratches around their necks and ears, and kissed each one above their wrinkly and stuffed up noses. "Love you little turds," she said and turned, exiting the house. She had to exit the back door being that the front door had only one ancient key to the house; clearly not practical if there is more than one person in the home. Previous tenants clearly thought so as well and made a more modern back door lock with normal keys, so there were spares. From the back porch, she could see the blue of the water and the grey of the morning. She liked being so close to water and thought how lucky Jo was to have this view. It was peaceful and beautiful. The house, on the other hand, was questionable. She walked from the back of the house, up the side driveway, and out toward the front and started running in the direction of the shopping center. As she jogged, she thought of the night before and the strangeness and the craziness of it all, of how frightening it was and even her mind questioned if it happened at all – although she knew it did.

The cool morning kept her from dripping sweat but she was misting and after a few minutes she was at the café. She slowed down a bit before to reduce her heart rate. Wiping the sweat off her brow she entered Mamma's and Ginni saw her immediately, greeting her with a big smile in the same spot she left her last time, behind the counter at the espresso machine.

"Hey, cutie," Ginni yelled out at her. "It's 9 am, you're late!"

"I never told you what time I was coming in. I only said morning," she replied sagaciously with a smile.

"I can take a break," Ginni replied finishing up a drink.

"You just got here an hour ago," a low energy, young, male co-worker stated.

Ginni looked at him as though he insulted her. "Consider it an opportunity to shine," she said into his neck and smiled a fake smile and tossed her towel at him, which he caught. "Besides, I work overtime here all the time and pick up shifts for everyone, so stop your bitchin','" she said jokingly. Her coworker smiled as though this was a common sort of banter, they hurled at each other playfully. No feelings were hurt.

Ginni went around the counter and instantly hugged Layce and pushed her face into her neck affectionately and then swung to her side and locked arms with her, walking toward the door.

"But I wanted coffee and a muffin," Layce whined longingly and looking back at all the possible things she could be eating.

"Don't worry," Ginni said reassuringly. "We're coming back and I'll feed you." Ginni smiled at her, almost flirtatiously with her face very close to hers.

Layce smiled at her. "Where are we going?" she probed.

"I'm taking you to the Spa."

"I don't want to go to a spa. I work in a spa."

"Oh? Rub my neck, it hurts," Ginni said jokingly knowing she must get that all the time.

Layce tilted her head down disapprovingly at her.

"I'm taking you to the animal spa and shelter."

"Uh, why?"

"I want you to meet Rico, my man."

"What! Why would I want to meet him?" she said laughing. "He's probably 'a real douche','" she exclaimed quoting from the movie *Nacho Libre*.

126

"What," Ginni said laughing. She knew it was all in fun and kept her arms locked with Layce all the way to the dog spa.

Layce felt a little crush on Ginni and it seemed, from her flirtations and affection, that she was feeling it too. Why she was taking her to meet the boyfriend she wasn't sure, but she went with it. They stopped in front of the spa.

"Ruff Times and Happy Endings—Transitional Dog Spa," Layce read the sign out loud. "Haha, Happy Endings and Spa. Nice pun," she announced dryly, but smiling. She did think it was cute.

"This is where Jo got the dogs. Rico helped her. That's my boyfriend."

Layce's eyebrows went up. "Oh," she said in a high pitch voice pretending to care.

Ginni just laughed, locked into her sarcasms and facial expressions. It was strange how easily they spoke to one another and understood all their playful tones, never mistaking them for serious comments when others probably would. It was as though they had known one another before. It was comfortable.

Ginni opened the door and Rico was at the front desk.

"Hey, girl," he said, busily processing files. "I'm a little busy," and they looked around the waiting area and could see almost every chair full with prospective new adoptive parents, with dogs coming and going.

"I see," she said and smiled. "Just wanted you to meet a newcomer to Gig." And she looked at Layce who was still locked in her arm.

Rico looked at Ginni and smiled, as though in on something and reached out to Layce to shake her hand.

"Nice to meet you, Rico," Layce said with a genuine smile and shook his hand. "I love the dogs you helped my sister find."

He asked, "Sister?"

"Jo," she replied. "She took three bulldogs from the spa."

"Oh," he said with a higher inflection. "Jo's your sister, wonderful! She is a great gal. Funny, too!" he said with a smile. "Well, ladies, I have to get working. So nice to meet you Layce, and Gin, I'll see you later. Lunch at one?"

"Yah, that sounds good," she said smiling at him, and she and Layce left the spa.

Outside Ruff Times Ginni began walking her back toward Mamma's.

"Food now, please!" Layce requested, half whimpering, half demanding.

Still arm in arm Ginni looked at her face, leaned in, foreheads touching and said, "Yes, now I will feed you." And they walked back.

Layce beamed at the affectionate gesture. "I want a regular coffee with stevia and a coffee cake muffin."

Ginni squeezed her chin gently, "OK, you shall have it," and she smiled. As they entered, she smelled the amazing scent of potatoes, peppers and onions mixed with sweet breads. Ginni walked her into the dining room and had her take a seat. "I'll be right back, your highness, with your items before you have a meltdown." Ginni walked away looking back and smiling at her.

Layce could see her at the coffee station getting her muffin and watched her walk back to her. She liked Mamma's Cafe, it was homey, safe and smelled delicious. Ginni placed everything she asked for in front of her and sat next to her in the booth. Something she didn't expect, so she scooted over slightly.

"You don't have to go far," Ginni exclaimed grabbing her knee.

Layce smiled and stayed but turned toward her to talk. She picked at her muffin and broke it into pieces as she ate and drank coffee. "Perfect," she said content with the taste.

"Good. So what do you think of Rico?"

"Oh, uh, he's nice?"

Ginni laughed.

"Did you introduce me so I would know the person I was gonna steal you from?" Layce said boldly.

Ginni could do nothing else but laugh at her straightforwardness. She never responded, only leaned in toward her and then back again with a coy intrigue.

Sufani Weisman-Garza

"OK, I'm waking up now, so I want to tell you about what happened last night. It was freaky. First though, do you believe in ghosts?"

Ginni's face changed and got serious. "Oh, my God. Tell me."

Twenty-One

Having ended the appointment early with Dr Donovan, Jo was in her car steadily heading toward her latest google map mark; Gig Harbor Peninsula Historical Society. She felt a little sad that she wasn't really going to be seeing Doc Donovan but felt that she needed the space. Life was offering her other things to focus on other than her grief, and now that her sister was here and Mother coming in the next morning, she didn't need extra things getting in the way of her flow to get things done around the house, and to visit with her family. She would deal with her grief in her own way, in her own time.

Pulling into the driveway she looked at the beautiful yet reserved building and made her way inside. It was quiet, as one would expect. She felt the pull to be silent and yet a little in awe of the knowledge that must be contained within. It was like that feeling of being in a court building. knowing it is filled with learned people who know stacks of laws you are clueless about or haven't even heard of; that feeling of feeling small in something immense and powerful. She saw a woman by a very nice, old, heavy desk, standing in the rear of the room and walked toward her. A nice plump woman, in her mid to late sixties she guessed. She had a sweet face and nice demeanor.

"Hello, dear. How may I help you?" she asked pleasantly.

Sufani Weisman-Garza

"Hi. I recently bought the old Victorian house on 1377 Rikoppe Lane." She paused to see if there was any reaction. There wasn't, so she continued. "I was wondering if I can get any information about the house."

"OK. Let me look in the back to see what we have." Within minutes, she came back with a book and a bundle of other items that seemed to contain an old-fashioned census of sorts, sophisticated for the times. "Firstly, my name is Geraldine." And she held out her hand to introduce herself properly.

"Jo Williams," and she smiled returning the gesture. "Nice to meet you."

"Likewise, Jo Williams," she said and led them to a table to sit down at. "It shows here that there have been only three owners of your home in all, before you." And she looked up and smiled. "Of course, with the invention of the computer in the twentieth century everything switched over, dear." And she looked up from the book and smiled. She had brown hair and pretty curls in a pull up do and wore very soft coral colored lipstick that gave her a sweet and warm feeling. She had old fashioned cats' eye spectacles hanging from a classy, beaded necklace. Used for close up reading Jo imagined.

"What can you tell me about the house?" Jo asked out of curiosity.

Geraldine e pulled out some other papers from a large book-like folder and found what she was looking for.

"It shows here that the house was built in 1890 by a Doctor Arthur Purdy. He was a dentist." And she pointed at the information on the form, inviting Jo to take a look. "It says that he had a wife and a child," she said smiling, as though they solved a riddle. "After that, there was the Minter family and after that," she said pointing at the document, "the Vaughn family. These families kept the home within their lineage well beyond the original owners, their parents, which means that they were passed down to children, before being sold to the next owner. That was quite common in those days. Sure would help out a lotta folks today if that same tradition lived on; you know passing down a family home, that is," she said clarifying. "Nowadays they just sell and split the profits." And she closed the book. "Don't you just feel a difference in a home that has been loved for generations by a family who's had multiple generations in the home?" And she looked at Jo.

"Yes, it definitely does have a different feel than say an apartment, or new home."

They both smiled in agreement.

"Is there anything else about the home that I need to know? Any tragedies, or anything?" Jo said casually, asking for more information.

Geraldine's face changed to consideration. She studied Jo's face for a moment. "Is there a reason, my dear, you would be guided to think that something had?" she continued with a concentrated, inquisitive look, her tone digging to inquire more.

"Well," Jo hesitated, "the house," she said, looking around uncomfortably, "it… well, strange things are happening in it, that I can't really explain, and I was just wondering." And then she was interrupted by Geraldine.

"If there was a ghost in your house?"

Jo laughed and felt silly. "Yes, I suppose I was just looking for some other explanation. The things occurring, they are *really* strange and, well, scary, Geraldine. I'm looking for answers, basically."

"Scary?" Geraldine pried further.

"Paranormal," Jo vaguely explained.

After a moment of silence, Geraldine continued, "Well, these papers here will not give all that detail. I can do some more research to see if I can find anything else. One thing I can tell you, though, is that the house was built shortly after the town was plotted. Doctor Purdy was here just after Gig Harbor was actually plotted in 1888. So, we have records on the home. As I stated, it stayed with family for a long, long time.. People were settled in the area before Gig Harbor was plotted out you see. People settled all over, wherever they could, and groupings of people became towns, and towns became cities as they grew. The larger a community, the more records began to be necessary. The Purdy family clearly updated the records with their name as records became necessary and required with development."

"I see. That's interesting. Okay, well if you could look into it, and if you find anything you think I might want to know, please give me a call." Jo handed her an old business card that had her cell phone number on it. "The cell number is still accurate."

Geraldine looked down at the card showing her last title was in a marketing position. "You're no longer at this business?"

"No, taking time off." Jo winked at Geraldine. Her face must have shown some sadness because Geraldine's energy immediately changed into that of a comforting mother.

"I understand," she said to Jo, who had not revealed anything.

"I lost my husband, too. You didn't have to say anything. It's deeply embedded in the face in certain facial expressions. I guess it takes one to know one," she said in a more chipper tone and went on to carry the documents toward her desk. Geraldine casually shared something of herself that bound them together – their experience.

"I suppose," Jo responded. "Well, it was nice meeting you Geraldine. Do you mind if I visit you again in the future if I have any questions?"

"You may visit me even if you do not have any questions, my dear." And she looked up from her desk and cats' eye glasses with a smile. "Come for tea sometime. When you have settled in, let's discuss the national registry for your house, dear. Much has been done already."

"Oh, okay, yes, I'm not quite ready for that discussion yet. Tea, I'm ready for though." Jo smiled and waved goodbye as she walked out and back to her car. Although she had learned more about her home, she had not come away with anything that could explain anything really. Just informative information about the lineage of who had once owned the place. It was interesting but offered no clues. The best thing she could do now was move on and could start by decorating the cold room with Layce. She had to stop putting it off and she could use a fun distraction. She texted Layce that she was on the way home before she got into the car. When she got home, she saw that Layce had texted her in return that she was still with Ginni with a few other bulletins on how cute Ginni was, and that Ginni seemed to be flirting with her. Jo looked at the messages and just shook her head laughing, as she took out the ancient key and opened the front door and went in. The dogs were nowhere to be found on the first level, which was very odd, being that they had trouble up the stairs and typically stayed downstairs during the day and went up only at night with her. She instantly began to look for them. Where were the dogs?

Twenty-Two

Within minutes, Layce came back to the house. Being that she knew Jo was home and the door would be unlocked she came in the front of the house. Immediately she was greeted by the dogs barking and happy to see her. She scratched them and yelled out to Jo she was home. There was no response, and the house was quiet. Looking around, she looked out the back door window to see Jo perched on the first step, smoking a clove, and wiping away tears. Layce froze and put her hand on the door window quietly, determining what to do. With Jo's resilience, she often forgot her sister was human and not always a superpower. She had just experienced the suicide of her husband, and Layce needed to remember that, despite how tough Jo was. She could not imagine how painful that must be for Jo. She allowed Jo another minute to wipe her tears. Jo was not a sobber for the most part. Much worse, she would sob silently to herself and because of that no one ever understood how much pain she was really in. She was a silent crier. One thing she learned from Jo was that you could spot a silent crier, because their tears would exit their eyes from the sides. This was due to holding them back as long as possible. She had waited long enough. She opened the door.

"Jo," she said quietly and sensitively, looking at her face and then sitting next to her. Layce put her arm around

137

her but did not say a word. What could she say, she knew what it was and there was no way out of the pain, but through it. They were silent for many minutes and just looked out onto the water from the back garden and at all the pretty ferns that seem to be able to survive the winter and the unused servants' quarters that until now had only been used for storage. Layce hadn't even seen it yet. "I'm here, Sis," Layce said, sitting by her sister's side and rocking her back and forth.

Jo smiled and continued to look out.

"I was thinking," Layce said changing the subject. "I could move here with you and just not go back."

Jo looked at her. "You would do that, Layce?" She was surprised by the offer.

"Of course, Sis. Home is where family is. I can get a job out here, easy. You shouldn't be alone."

"And?" Jo said, smiling, knowing there was an additional motive.

"And Ginni is nice," Layce said with an ear-to-ear smile.

They both laughed. Attraction was a good motivator and yet, she still understood that Layce was really staying for her, Ginni was just a lucky bonus. Who knew where that would go? Layce just enjoyed change and adventure and honestly, Jo needed her there.

"Sis, that would be great," Jo said. "Call today if you want to let them know you're not coming back and give your roommates notice. I could really use you here to help me with stuff and just to have you here. I could use family with me right now." Her eyes got watery and she looked away.

"I'm not going anywhere, Sis."

"By the way, did you go into the cold room this morning before you left and leave the door open? Because I found the dogs huddled up in there by the windows with the door shut? They must have clumsily closed the door," Jo said as she put out the cigarette. When she looked up, she saw Layce's face of confusion.

"When I left, the dogs were downstairs at the door seeing me off, and I didn't go into that room, sister, I swear!"

Their eyes became deeply fixed on each other and didn't say a word. They were afraid of what those words would mean.

Twenty-Three

Leaving the porch, they both stood up and entered the back of the house. The dogs scuffled, probably wondering what they were doing out there on the porch.

"Let's get upstairs now and go to the cold room," Jo said.

Layce looked at her, not saying anything.

"We have to start work on that room and look inside that huge walk-in closet. I don't even know what's in there, but I want to try to brighten up the mood."

"I agree. We need to figure out what's going on with that room and why it feels heavier," Layce offered. "Do you think it's because of the wood choice in the cabinetry?" she asked rationally as they walked toward the room.

"It could be that," Jo pondered. "I thought that myself. But still, I don't understand why it is cold when the heat runs through the whole house. I think we should look at the vents too, to make sure none of them are closed," she said, looking at Layce, as she put her hand on the doorknob and twisted, opening the door to the room.

"Good idea," Layce said, and they both looked into the room before entering for some strange reason. The shadows of the trees cast light across the hardwood floor and the breath of the room was chilling. It was cold, the way a room gets cold that is rarely opened and has nowhere to go but in the bones of the room. The built-ins

140

of the room spoke of a time long ago and created a sense of needing to be quiet in its presence to honor the dead. It did not give the feeling of permission for someone to turn on a radio and dance in their pajamas. It silenced you like a morgue; a feeling that Jo wanted to change in the room. There was no reason at all that the room should be like that, and she intended to change it; to make it warm again.

"Do you think you need to trim the tree back to get more light in?" Layce asked as they both entered the room rather cautiously, and for no apparent reason.

They ventured toward the window, which felt natural. Perhaps just like the dogs did? Perhaps it was because, like the door, it offered hope of escape?

The walls, the floors, the décor, the curtains, all screamed of lavishness, elite extravagance of past times and yet there was a poverty in the room somewhere unseen. Something felt off, wrong in the beauty and it was a contradiction that was not visible, and so they continued with their task.

"Before we bring everything up from the guest house, we need to get into that closet and move out anything that is there to store," Jo said.

"Is there anything in there?" Layce said with trepidation.

"I don't know," Jo responded "I never went in there. It's fricken dark in here and I wasn't gonna go in there alone," she exclaimed.

Layce nodded her head in understanding, no questions asked.

Jo pulled open the two solid wood doors of the closet that ran floor to ceiling in the immense built-in, walk-in closet made of solid wood. The door was open and yet it allowed no entrance of light from the natural light in the room. It was as if they were staring into a black abyss or another dimension to where nothing became apparent until one entered it.

Jo turned on the vanity light by the sink just outside the bathroom, but the large door blocked the light. She turned on the bathroom light, but the light was set back against the other wall and shed no light into the room far enough to soak up the darkness of the closet. Nothing worked.

Again, they were silenced to a whisper.

"Is there a light in there?" Layce asked her sister, putting her head closer to Jo's while looking into the darkness.

Neither of them moved.

"Yes, I believe so. I mean, mine has one. A pully; those little silver beaded ones. It's in the middle of the closet."

"Go turn it on," Layce whispered.

Jo looked at her like she was crazy. Whispering in answer, she said, "You must be joking! I'm not going in that." And she looked again at the black pit. "I'll get a flashlight," she said, and they both backed up slowly not turning their back to it and when close to the hallway door they turned and walked out of the room. Jo went to the old laundry service station where there was a desk, and built-in cabinets for linens and found the flashlight she had put in the drawer. They walked back to the room and once again were standing side by side looking into the darkness of the closet.

"It seems pretty deep in there," Layce offered.

"Yah, they're pretty big," Jo answered, distracted by her anxiety to turn on the light. As she flipped on the flashlight, they both breathed a sigh as they saw a closet much the same as their own, but there were webs, some boxes laying around and old hangers. They walked in and Jo pulled the light string to turn the light on. It smelled musty and damp.

"I'm gonna get the broom to get these cobwebs out," Layce proclaimed in a spirit of helpfulness while Jo looked at boxes on the floor to see what they were. She wondered why boxes were left from the previous owners. It seemed strange they did not take them.

The broom was not far away and Layce had come right back and began taking down the cobwebs with the broom. "These webs are old, Sis," Layce volunteered. "It's like no one's been in here for ages or something," she said working on, though confused.

"Or they just stayed out of this room much like we

143

did," Jo replied.

While Layce worked on the webs, Jo opened up a box in the corner. It had old fashioned children's clothing and pieces of hair clippings tied on strings.

"Look at this." Jo showed Layce, holding up a lock of hair with a bow tied to it.

Layce's face crunched up. "That's weird. Why did people do that? That's baby hair. Didn't that baby need that hair?" Layce said in a scolding manner. "I don't get it."

"That's an old custom, to cut hair and locks this way. Some people probably still do it. Mom probably has some of ours. But a lot of people think it's weird now. Sometimes they did this when a person would die, to have a piece of their person as a reminder to them. They even did family photos with the dead person all dressed up and posed." Immediately after she said that, she paused, they both did. Was the lock in her hand a piece of hair from a dead person or worse, a dead child? And why the hell was it in this house in the closet, left behind by an old resident. And why were there several?

"I'm gonna see if Marshall," she looked at Layce, "the realtor I use, can communicate to the past owners that they left a box, so I can send this out. They must want this stuff." She looked no further in the boxes and just pushed them out of the closet to be taken down to the guest house outside the house to deal with later. "We'll take these out after we clean up in here," Jo announced.

Layce continued with taking down the webs and then began sweeping the floor. They both looked down at a piece that was discolored in the back corner of the closet where the markings of a claw foot had indented it. It somewhat preserved the floor by covering it leaving a fresher appearance than the more trafficked area of the hardwood. "Do you see that?" Layce asked, knowing that she did.

They looked at each other.

"We have to look," Layce said and did not continue. She knew Jo understood what she meant. They walked over to the floor and Jo stepped on it. It let out a creak. The pieces of the floor were flush. It would require a knife. As Jo got up to go get one, the door to the closet unexpectedly slammed shut.

Jo's heart raced with what-ifs in an instant and she rushed to the door, turning the knob feverishly to no avail. She turned to look at Layce, whose eyes were bugged, scared silent. Just then the door opened to her insistent turns, and they sighed.

Layce became angry. "OK, I'm out of here. This is ridiculous." And she stomped out of the door, Jo followed behind and they both pushed shut the doors. "I don't even give a crap about what's in those boxes, or under that wooden plank. Can we please just bring the furniture in and do our do here, and then get out of this room, please?"

Jo responded nodding her head in fierce agreement.

Sufani Weisman-Garza

"Absolutely."

And they both walked downstairs to go toward the back of the house to go to the guest house outside to bring in the mattresses and room items. Adding the bed and the beautiful sheets, comforter, and pillows in the traditional floral patterns, made the room feel more Victorian than she thought it might. Jo was very good at decorating, better than she had thought within this era. She knew where every little table should go, how to add things to make a room feel soft, but not too many things to make it cluttered. No photos in rooms also made it feel like a B&B. It allowed people to enter it and feel as though they were creating their own memories, not living in someone else's. Within just a few hours, the room was completely put together, and it was well past lunch time. It had been a busy day. With the last item on the dresser put in place, they both stood by the door to the hallway entrance and looked at the landscape of the room.

Both smiling, Layce offered, "We did good!"

Jo nodded proudly. "Yah, we did."

Although they had done much to turn the room from its darkness, it still had the feeling, although no longer the appearance, of something darker, something colder in it. It was like they had covered it with a mask. Neither one of them wanted to acknowledge what they both instinctively already knew. The room was dark, and it would not be changed to anything other than that. It was

146

intrinsic, yet, not understood. They walked out of the room, and they closed the door behind them to go eat lunch. They both were happy to be out of the room for the day and away from whatever energy lurked there.

Twenty-Four

Lorna walked through the exit gate at the airport arm-in-arm with another older woman, chatting, smiling, and giggling together. Before she even looked out to see if her children were there, she hugged the woman and gave her a card with her number on it. "Make sure you call me, dear," she said, as the woman took the card and walked in the opposite direction, to her own family. Lorna looked up and around, as she adjusted her purse strap and spotted her lovely daughter. Lorna was a proud mother of her two daughters, Layce, and Jo. She was formidable, but very loving. She was the type of woman who would bake you apple pie and tuck you in at night, but mess with her kids and she was capable of ripping off your head. She was warm and friendly, and everyone loved her. Her hair was strawberry blonde and shiny. It suited her personality that was also like the sunshine. She was sensitive, but hardy enough to wrangle her girls, all on her own after the death of her husband. She was strong, and yet knew how to be soft. Softness was her strength. Her love and dedication to her children was unparalleled.

Once she noticed the girls, her arms went up. "Oh my goodness! There are my girls," The girls ran to her, and they all embraced at the same time. Lorna pulled away and inspected Jo to make sure she was alright, particularly with the concern of a mother whose daughter had just endured a tragedy. "Let me look at you, Johannah," she said, touching her hair and backing her away slightly by holding her shoulders as she inspected her. "You look marvelous. The move has done you good."

"Yah, if you like ghosts," Layce said under her breath with a snicker.

"What, dear?" Lorna asked pleasantly.

Jo's eyes got big at her as Lorna was looking at Layce, signaling her to keep her mouth shut about the things in the home. Lorna was sensitive anyway and if there were anything there, she would know it on her own.

Layce smiled. "Oh nothing, Mom. She is doing great. I'm moving here with her."

"What?" her mother said ecstatically. "Layce," she paused and looked at her daughter with delight, "that is just a wonderful thing you're doing for your sister. You're a good person." She pointed her finger three times at Layce's chest gently. They all smiled. "I've missed you girls. With Layce gone this last week, I've been busy with friends, but I need my daughters. I can't be away from you for long."

"Mom, you can move in with me too. The house is huge."

Lorna put her arms around both of the girls' waists and began to guide them to walk in the direction of baggage claim. "Oh, you know I love my little apartment and I have all my friends there. Besides, I'm dating someone right now."

Heads turned.

"What?" both the girls said at the same time. Their mother had not had a real, soulful relationship since their father died. Well, not that they ever knew about, and it was time for her to get on with her life.

"Yes, he's quite dapper. He looks like Cary Grant, the grey version. He wears those big thick glasses too and looks hot!" she said, as she giggled. She was still getting used to being more free and expressive.

"Mom?" Layce said like a little girl who couldn't believe her mother was a sexual being.

"Oh, Layce, get over it. Mom is a person, just like us. Why don't you tell her how you're trying to steal Ginni from her boyfriend?"

Shocked, Layce just said, "Wha…?" and made a face at her to keep some secrets.

"Up to your old tricks again, huh?" Lorna replied with amusement.

Reaching the baggage claim area, they found that the suitcases were already circulating.

"Wow, are they fast around here! Small town, I guess. Never get that kind of service in Orange County. Everyone takes their sweet time getting your bags out there." Lorna spotted her bag. "Ooh, there's mine." She pointed to a pink bag with leopard print pockets.

Jo laughed. "Mom, you're too much." And she leaned over and grabbed her medium sized bag.

Lorna was a profound person with the air of simplicity. She was low maintenance. She wasn't the kind who over-packed or claimed low maintenance status but was high maintenance. She didn't like to make a fuss over things, she packed what she needed and things that would be versatile to save space, she stayed away from drama, when there was a problem, she solved it and when people were sad and holding on to things, she helped them laugh and let go. Lorna was truly a beautiful person inside and out and made friends with just about everyone she came in contact with. That trait used to bother Layce, who always seemed to be rushing from one event to the next and was bothered by her mother's constant interruption to her speed demon personality, by talking to others. Layce grew out of that irritation and learned to love that about her mother later. Her mother never changed and never saw the need to. She loved interacting and that was her way of giving healing to the world.

"Mom," Jo said as she grabbed her bag, and they began to walk towards the doors to leave baggage claim. "We made the downstairs room nice for you and you have your own bathroom." Jo looked at Layce creasing her brow to not make any wise crack like, 'Yah, hope yours isn't haunted'. Layce didn't say a word. "It's also close to the kitchen and of course, the library and family room."

Lorna took Jo's face in her hands sweetly and just smiled and took a deep breath. "Thank you, dear. Let's get

151

home now." They all agreed and went straight to the car.

"Hungry, Mom?" Layce asked.

Jo shot Layce a look, seeing right through her. She wanted to see Ginni.

"Oh, sure, I could eat. All they had were stale muffins and raisins on the plane. They were hard anyway," Lorna exclaimed.

"Good, let's go to Mamma's Coffee Shop," Layce said excitedly. Her tail would be wagging if she had one.

"If it's alright with your sister," Lorna said fiddling with something in her purse, as she sat in the front seat, with Layce in the back, pushing her head in between the two front seats with child-like enthusiasm.

"Sure, I could eat too, and I need coffee," Jo said.

Without skipping a beat Lorna said, "And then you can show me your Ginni who clearly works at Mamma's Coffee Shop," winking in her direction.

Layce just smiled at her mother affectionately and they drove on. First stop, Mamma's Coffee Shop. This was becoming a habit.

Twenty-Five

The three of them walked into Mamma's Coffee Shop, and instantly Layce spotted Ginni and her face showed disappointment. Her mother looked at her and then at what she was looking at. Layce was looking at Ginni, but not just Ginni, Ginni sitting and having coffee with Rico, her boyfriend. Her mother looked at her and laughed, saying nothing. Ginni noticed they all walked in and Ginni knew that their mother was coming into town. Ginni quickly got up and made her way to them to say hello. Ginni looked at Layce first and smiled and then at Jo.

"This must be the lovely mother?" and she held out her hand to greet Lorna.

Lorna smiled and extended her hand. "Hello, dear. And you must be Ginni?" and she looked at Layce and smiled and then back to Ginni as she shook her hand.

"Yes, it's true," and she shook her head up and down, returning her hand to her hip.

Layce said nothing, clearly perturbed by seeing her future girlfriend with her current boyfriend.

Still standing, Jo asked, "Is it okay if we just grab a table? We want to get a bite and then get Mom back to the house and settled in."

"Of course. Anywhere you like and then I will be right with you," Ginni said enthusiastically.

"OK, great," Jo said and smiled, as they walked into

153

the dining room.

Ginni continued to look at Layce as Jo and Lorna walked on. Layce did not return the glance at Ginni. Ginni's face sank a little. Then as Ginni stood there she cheered up. It was obvious that Layce was jealous. Ginni smiled and laughed a little under her breath, as though she thought it was cute. "Hey, Layce, don't you go changin' to try to please me," Ginni yelled out, quoting the lyrics to the Billy Joel song, as she walked away. Layce looked back and couldn't help a smirk.

"I'll deal with you later," she said in a sarcastic and jocular whisper, pointing her finger at her. Ginni smiled, and just like that their first argument was over.

They ate their meal and had their coffee and then said their goodbyes to Ginni. Rico had long since left when they had gotten there. He finished his bagel and coffee and most likely had returned to the dog spa and shelter.

Layce lagged behind as Jo and Lorna walked out. Layce was about to walk out and was pulled back in by Ginni. Ginni held her fingers and although she had pulled her back in already, she did not let go of her hand.

"Are we okay, love bug?" Ginni asked.

"Maybe," Layce returned, still somewhat pouting. Ginni shook her head. "I guess we're going to have to talk about this at some point."

"This, being our attraction?"

Ginni nodded.

"Well, I will say this. There's one too many of us at this party. My sister needs me now," she said abruptly cutting the conversation short. "And I don't really want to get involved in any drama. I'm a peaceful sort of person. Crazy, but peaceful."

"Strange combination," Ginni offered. Their stance was close, Layce's body language suddenly standoffish. Layce shook her head and pushed open the door again to leave but smiled at her.

"But I like it, Ginni,' she said as she walked out. Ginni looking a little bewildered, as though her life had just gotten complicated.

Twenty-Six

They got into the house and Jo showed her mother her room.

"Goodness gracious, look at the view," she said, looking at Jo and then at Layce. They both smiled. Layce beamed with total agreement with how amazing it was to look out from the window of her bedroom and the back door and be able to see the harbor.

"This view is a privilege, you know," Lorna said, looking back at Jo from the window.

"Yes, Mom, I do have to agree." And she went to the window quietly and looked out.

Her mother sat on the bed and bounced a little looking around at the decorations and then back at her daughter. Jo had changed ever so slightly – her words were just a little heavier, her light a little darker. "Layce, my lovely, will you get me a glass of water," she asked and winked at her.

Layce looked at Jo who was still looking out and said, "Sure, Mom," understanding that her mother wanted a moment alone with Jo.

"How are you doing, baby girl?"

Jo turned from the window and smiled. "I'm good, Mom. Don't you worry about me."

"Jo," Lorna said firmly. "You come sit here." And she tapped the space next to her on the mattress. Jo complied

156

with her mother's wishes. "Tell me how you are really doing, daughter. And don't give me any crap about it!"

Jo laughed and looked at her mother who still had the tone of a mother whom you did not say no to. "I'm sad sometimes. I'm keeping myself busy with the house and with Layce and the dogs, and now you," she said and smiled at her mother.

Lorna shook her head listening. "Are you allowing yourself to grieve, Jo?"

"Yes, I think so. I've been grieving for a while, Mom, and I don't think wallowing is going to help me. I've never been that way, and I don't intend to start. I pick myself up and move on, and that's what I am doing. When I feel sad, I'm sad. I saw a doctor and that helped me get adjusted."

"Oh?" Lorna inquired.

"Yah, he was very nice, and it did help me get acclimated to the new place. He actually knew of the kids but they weren't close."

Just then Layce walked in with the water. "And he's hot, Mom."

"Layce," Jo said plaintively.

"What? He is!" Layce confirmed.

"Is this true, Jo?" Lorna smiled.

"Yes, he is empirically nice looking. Oh, I did also run into him at the farmers' market too. He lives near here, he said, so we shop in the same area. I'm sure we'll eventually run into him out and about some day and you'll get to

Sufani Weisman-Garza

meet him," Jo explained.

"Oh, that would be nice. I'd like to thank him for making my daughter feel at home in her new town." And Lorna touched Jo's cheek and then got up to fiddle with opening her suitcase.

Layce handed over the water. "Mom, unpack and get comfy here and when you come out, we'll show you the rest of the house."

"OK, girls, sounds good," she said, not looking up but putting her clothes into the dresser.

Layce and Jo stepped out of the room and instantly Jo wondered where the dogs were. They both walked down the hallway toward the front of the house.

"Are we gonna tell Mom about the house?" Layce said in a soft voice, as they moved down the hall.

"Not right away, Layce. Let's just let her settle in and hope the house behaves."

"Mom is pretty sensitive anyway, Jo. I bet we don't need to say anything, and Mom will pick up on it. I bet you."

Jo shook her head and then stepped in front of the library. "Did you shut the pocket doors to the library?" she asked Layce.

"I didn't even know there were pocket doors there." Jo opened the doors, and the dogs were safely lying on the couch and one on the rug in front of the couch, as usual. Their heads all came up and Ferrah jumped down to see her mommy.

158

"Aw, hi, baby girl. How are you?" she said and scratched her neck, as Ferrah snorted and breathed hard. The boys got up slower and made their way over to Jo and Layce for some love. Jo looked up at Layce. "You didn't?"

Layce didn't say a word, she just shook her head no. They didn't discuss it, they just moved on.

"Do you guys want to meet my mom?" she said to the dogs. They shook and snorted and jumped, and she took that as a yes. She stood up, and they walked back towards Lorna's room, taking the lead. Jo peeked in her mother's room, but she was not there.

"Where is sh —" stopping mid word. She had turned around and saw the dogs staring up the stairs. Jo looked at Layce who pursed her lips.

"Mom?" Jo yelled out, as she climbed the steps. There was no response. Layce followed closely behind; the dogs remained downstairs. Whether it was because they were lazy, or they had good reason was unknown. Layce followed closely behind Jo. There was no noise upstairs at all. She yelled out again. "Mom," this time a little more softly, as though she did not want the house to hear.

At the top of the stairs, Layce and Jo stood on the landing at the farthest end of the hall. Their mother was not in the hallway either. Jo looked back down at the dogs, still standing silently, only looking up at her. It was strange the way they were motionless, all of them. They went down the hallway peeking into Layce's room whose door

Sufani Weisman-Garza

was always open and needn't look at Jo's room because as they got closer, they saw the door to the cold room open. It was not fully open, only a quarter of the way, so that they could only see the windows facing out, but not the interior of the room.

"Mom," Jo said with trepidation and placed her hand on the door pushing it open a little more, as it creaked and gave way. Lorna was standing in front of the closet, as if they had just interrupted something.

"Mom, everything okay?"

Lorna looked at the curio cabinet. "The strangest thing happened."

Jo and Layce looked at each other.

"What, Mom, what happened?" Layce said, coming to her and placing her hand on her shoulder. The mother's demeanor was quiet and pondering.

"I heard a voice at the top of the stairs, and it didn't sound like either of you, so I popped my head out of my room. There was a woman in her forties standing there in an old-fashioned white dress, waving me to come up the stairs. I thought you guys had let her in or something, maybe a friend of yours."

Layce and Jo listened intently ,and Jo shook her head.

"No one came in. We didn't let anyone in, Mom," Layce said.

"Well," she said looking again at the closed closet door. "She walked with me down the hall. Nice lady. She opened this door and said, 'It happened here'. She said there was a lot of history in this house, and that '*it*' happened in here. I kept asking her what happened and tried to get her to tell me. She touched my hand and said, 'Be careful, please, be careful', and she looked at the closet, so I looked. Just then you both came in and when I turned around, she was gone."

"Oh, Mom." Jo was overwhelmed and went and sat on the bed. She looked at Layce. "Did she hurt you, or scare you in anyway," Jo said, first and foremost checking on her mother.

"Oh! No, dear. She seemed nice and gentle with me. There was something different about her from the beginning, I felt it. The sort of feeling you get when you feel you should whisper. Our interaction was so quiet. Now that I think about it, Jo, I don't know if I was even actually speaking, and yet we had a conversation. I thought she was real, but she wasn't, was she?"

Jo sighed very deeply and looked at the closet. "Mom, something, I don't know, I think something happened here. We should tell you everything that has happened up to now. We didn't want to talk to you just yet about it until you settled in. But it looks like we must now. Um, let's go downstairs and have some tea and sweet rolls and we'll bring you up to date. I want to get out of this room." Jo felt a chill and an air of murkiness to the environment.

Sufani Weisman-Garza

They all began to walk out.

"Jo," Lorna said, stopping at the door of the room and looking back. "Whatever it was, she said it happened in here. And she looked frightened," she said, looking at Jo. "I felt like she was warning us of something in here." She gave another look at the room that was very beautiful on inspection, but felt somehow subdued, some other energy silently looking. Something was heavy in that room and of concern even to the dead, even still. Lorna was the last to leave and turned around slowly closing the door. She looked toward the window and saw the figure of the woman, watching her close the door and encouraging her to do so. She did not say a word.

Twenty-Seven

"How long has this been going on?" Lorna asked as they all sat at the table.

Jo had put the tea kettle on, and as they waited, they sat around the table like they did when they were children, talking things over. The dogs had followed them to the kitchen, having never moved from the staircase the entire time the family was in the cold room. Even the dogs were leery of that room, and they waited to make sure that Jo, Layce, and the new person were safe.

"From the first night, I was here, Mom," and she continued to tell the story of every event that had taken place in the house since she had gotten there. Even of the most recent scare which seemed to have escalated to a more frightening level.

"Can you refund a house?" Layce asked. "You know, because they didn't disclose this issue, so you can move out and they just fix the paperwork?"

"Layce, you know it doesn't work that way. Of course I can't do that. We're not talking about a shirt here, it's a house. And besides, I'm not going anywhere! This is my house, and the history of this house is now in my safe keeping and I'm not going anywhere. So, whatever is in this house is going to have to get square with me, 'cause I ain't leaving!"

Lorna smiled. She understood that determination to

163

fight for what was right and for what was yours.

"That's right, Hun," Lorna said touching Jo's hand. The tea kettle whistled and Jo got up to get the tea. Layce looked uncertain.

"What do you guys want? I have black tea with coconut, white silver needle tea or green tea."

"Ooh, silver needle," Layce replied. "That's a rare tea."

Jo nodded her head. "It used to be offered only to the emperor. It's hand-picked only one month a year. It's really amazing. Mom?" Jo asked.

"I like coconut," Lorna said.

"OK, you got it." And Jo began preparing them. She only used organic loose teas and stuffed her own unbleached tea bags.

"So, what do we do now?" Lorna asked. Just as she did the doorbell rang.

Both Lorna and Layce looked up at Jo.

"I have no idea who that could be," she said to the inquiring eyes. "I'll check. You stay here. Layce, will you put the bags in the cups for me?" And she walked down the hall with the dogs in tow.

She opened the door to find Dr Donovan on her porch. He must have read her face.

"Surprised?" he said.

"I thought you didn't do house calls," Jo smiled. The sight of him was comforting and she noticed his handsomeness. She's never really paid attention to it before and it was a little disconcerting to her that she noticed it now.

"Only for special people," he said and smiled. "May I come in?"

Jo opened the door. "Of course. We're just having tea. Come on back and I'll introduce you to my family."

They walked along together in silence down the hall and the dogs followed. As they walked into the kitchen the two women's eyes lit up. They were not expecting a handsome man to walk into the kitchen.

"Everyone, this is Dr Tryent."

"Donovan, please," he said reaching out his hand to Layce who was the closest.

"You're the doctor?" Layce asked. "Wow!" She looked at Jo. "Bow-chica-wow-wow?"

"Layce," Jo scolded immediately, but laughs had already begun. Even the doctor giggled a little.

"This is my mother, Lorna." And she gestured to her, and he politely walked to her and shook her hand gently and gallantly.

"Very nice to meet you." His smile was sincere and his demeanor unassuming.

"Same here, doctor. I was just telling Jo today that I was hoping to run into you somewhere in town to tell you thank you."

His widened. "Oh? For?"

Sufani Weisman-Garza

Jo pulled out a chair for him to sit down and he did

"Tea?" she asked him.

"Yes, thank you."

Lorna continued, "For making my baby's adjustment here friendly and a little bit easier. You know she's had a hard time of it lately and she needed someone to make her feel more comfortable. From the sounds of it, you helped her. So, I wanted to thank you, doctor."

"Oh, please, really, call me Donovan. Jo is no longer seeing me as a patient, so I am just Donovan now," he said and smiled at her. She brought over his tea.

"What kind did he get?" Layce asked.

"Black with coconut. Is that okay?" she asked looking at him.

"Sure, of course! Sounds delicious!"

She placed it down and he looked at it and then smelled it.

"Mmm, smells wonderful," he said instantly.

"Do you need any stevia, or honey?" Jo asked.

"Whatia, or honey?" He smiled playfully and looked at her.

"Stevia. It's an herb that is naturally sugary tasting but not sugar, so it's a sugar substitute. It reminds me of sweet-n-low, but not manufactured in a lab. It's from a real plant."

"Oh, that's cool. I'm intrigued. I'll take the Ste-via," he said, making sure he remembered it right.

Jo shook her head and smiled at him, passing him the

packet and a spoon.

"So does he know about the house?" Lorna asked, having just found out herself.

Jo appeared anxious discussing it with others who were not her family. She didn't know the doctor's beliefs, or feelings on the matter. He was very professional when she spoke to him the day before, and she gathered no real insight into his personal beliefs. He was simply open with her in her own.

"Yes, he knows a little," she answered, not encouraging more discussion about it.

Layce pulled up a chair next to Donovan. "Well, Doc, what do you think? Are we all nuts?"

"Layce!" Jo chided. "He's here on a social visit. Don't make him therapise us schizophrenics." And she smirked and looked at him.

"Okay, I can clearly state that you, Jo, are not schizophrenic. Layce and Lorna," he said looking at them, "on appearances and the few minutes I have known you, I see no reason to believe that either of you are schizophrenic." He smiled, clearly enjoying the relaxed way in which they all talked and that he did not have to be their doctor.

"Well, Donovan, I can tell you that I have been here for a very short time and already I've had an experience in this house; my first day! I saw a woman upstairs in the room. What do you girls call it again?"

167

"The cold room," Layce answered.

"Why do you call it that?" Donovan asked.

"No matter what time of day, heat on, or not, that room stays cold. Eerily cold," Jo answered.

"OK, go on, Lorna," the doctor asked, interested in her story.

"Yes, she was in period clothing, and she seemed concerned for us."

There was an uneasy silence. They all took a sip of tea. "I tell you what," the doctor announced in a chipper tone, "the next time something happens in here, day or night, you call me, and I will come. I think I would need to get a sense of what is happening by being here at the time. Maybe there will be a feeling or something I can share, to understand it better. Or maybe I can just offer a rational explanation. I would like to help," he said looking first at Jo and then at the family.

"Doctor?" Jo said.

"Donovan," he quickly corrected.

"This would be as a ... friend? I mean, I'm not your patient any more, remember? You don't have to offer your time to this."

"I want to, Johannah." He said her name so caringly, soft, and genuine. They both just looked at each other and Jo shook her head, to allow him to do what he offered.

They went on to have sweet rolls and polite conversation about the town and soon the doctor had to

168

return to his office. He had stayed for a good hour. As Jo walked him to the door, he took a moment to pet Nos-Ferrah-Tu.

"They are so cute."

"Yep, my babies," she said. "Thanks for coming by Doc … Donovan," she corrected herself and smiled at him as she held open the door.

"I meant what I said. You're not my patient any more Jo, but I like you. You're a nice person and you've been through a lot. Besides, we live close, and it would be nice to be friends." He smiled whole-souled and held her gaze. "Anyway, have a good rest of the day and see you around. Call me when you need me." And he walked out and off the porch looking back at her as he walked down the steps. He waved when he got in the car. She stood with the door open waiting until he drove off. Waiting for someone to enter their home or watch them leave was a politeness that she learned a long time ago and it never changed, although the world had drastically. She turned around to find Layce and Lorna standing behind her at the library.

"Oh my God, what a babe," Layce explained with jubilance.

Jo smiled but said nothing. Her mother just smiled, nodding her head. "I have to agree, Jo. He's *very* handsome and tall too. Even though he is a doctor, he seems very accessible. You know, not distant, I mean."

Jo nodded her head in agreement walking toward

them.

"You know how some doctors you just don't feel like you can really see who they are? Like they have on a mask or something. But Donovan, you could see his soul in his eyes. It was refreshing," Lorna explained.

The day had passed by pleasantly and it was time for bed. They did everything in a pack just to be safe and it was fun. They changed into their jammies and talked through the night until the wee hours of the night beckoned them all to sleep: first Lorna, then Layce and Jo was the last to enter her bedroom with the dogs. She went to bed and closed her eyes, still reminiscing about the good times when they were all together and her father was still alive She thought that good thought and fell asleep.

Twenty-Eight

Days had passed since Dr Donovan had visited Jo and her family. He couldn't stop thinking about their concern and the strange things happening in the house. He had just finished up with his last client of the day and was filling out some paperwork, but his mind kept returning to Johannah. He felt a connection with her from the first time he spoke with her on the phone. Like knowing someone for a long time, and even though time had passed, and distance has kept you away, the first reunion with the person felt as though not a day had passed. Jo felt familiar to him. He had never had anything paranormal happen to him, after all, his mind was trained in science. But he was not so arrogant, nor was his mind so closed to believe that just because he had not experienced anything, that it didn't exist. Although collectively his profession was under the impression that anyone who sees ghosts are usually schizophrenic, he believed life was perhaps a little more, even though he did not know what that more was. He understood that science did not yet have all the answers, although it tried to. The influence of his mother, a strict Catholic from Panama who believed in things she could not see and had her superstitions meant that he was not immune too. She held out the magic in life and some of that rubbed off on him. Although he did not espouse superstitions, he did not deny others their experience. He thought about Jo's experience and that maybe he should talk to his mother about the house and see what pearls she had for him to share with Jo and her family. It would also give him a reason to return to her home to see her. Although he knew she was still in mourning, he just wanted to see her again and be around her. He had no intention of trying to court her. But if and when the time was right in the future, he saw her as a worthy person to wait for. She didn't seem all that appalled by him either, he thought to himself. There was something nice between them, and at ease. He liked being in her company and felt at home. She seemed to feel comfortable too. But he couldn't know if that was only because she had once been his patient for a few sessions. Time would tell. Yes, he decided, after work he would stop by his mother's house and talk to her about the house. Perhaps she knew more than he did. He was just a kid growing up there around that house. She, however, had been around a lot longer to know the more adult stories of the town and perhaps she could shed some light.

Twenty-Nine

Layce woke up and did her morning run. She had gotten into the habit of stopping into Mamma's to get a coffee and walk back home. She had also started this new ritual because it allowed her to see Ginni. She did also need coffee and it kept her warm as her body cooled down. But this time she felt a little different entering knowing Ginni would be there. The way they left it, it became obvious that Ginni had a decision to make. She was not going to be in a love triangle. She avoided toxicity at all costs. She walked in and saw Ginni behind the expresso bar making drinks, steam billowing up around her. Ginni smiled but seemed a little uncomfortable.

"Hi," Ginni shouted out. "Hey."

Layce smiled.

"Your usual?"

"Yep. Please." She smiled at Ginni as she leaned up against the counter in a friendly manner, still smiling and feeling awkward and her expression became stale. Ginni had already seen her coming and poured her a cup of coffee to go which was her routine, but she asked her to be sure. She handed it to her and smiled.

"Oh. Thank you. I appreciate you having it ready." Layce put her money on the counter and raised her cup to Ginni. "Thank you." And she walked out of Mamma's. She had learned a long time ago that expectations hurt.

Sufani Weisman-Garza

She could do friendly, and friendly she would do.

Ginni continued making drinks, but looked at her as she walked away.

Thirty

"Is Layce here," Ginni asked when Jo opened her front door.

"Ginni, hi, hun. No, actually. She flew back to the Beach just about an hour ago. She didn't tell you?"

Ginni's face fell.

"Uh, come in, Ginni." Jo opened the door and ushered her to her left to sit in the living room. Ginni's face looked troubled, and she didn't want her to unload it all on the porch. She had the sneaking suspicion it had to do with Layce, because it always had to do with Layce. They both sat down across from each other, and just then the dogs ran in and sniffed and gave her love. She petted them and it seemed to cheer her up a little. "OK, spill it."

"Well, I saw Layce this morning. I wish she would have told me she was leaving."

Jo remained quiet.

"I'm…a little confused, I guess. I'm not sure how to handle this."

"This being?" Jo asked.

"Well, you know I'm with Rico," she said and looked up from her tennis shoes. "But I like Layce. I feel comfortable with her and we have a lot in common and we laugh a lot." She wandered off into thought.

"Well, do you have that with Rico?"

"No, not like that. I mean, we have a great friendship

Sufani Weisman-Garza

too, but the friendship I have with Layce is more connected, it feels like. And I am *very* attracted to Layce. More so than Rico, if I'm being honest." Her face looked a little guilty.

"Well, Ginni, you can't help that." Jo moved in closer to her and touched her knee. "Look, your body registers who you are attracted to in half a blink of an eye. That's a true scientific fact. That means that there is not really the element of thinking about it originally. It just is. Your body knows before you do. So it can't be helped. But I will say this, don't make a mess! Close one door before opening another. Don't muddy the water. If you have these thoughts about Rico, make it about that. Either way, focus on things in order. If Rico is ultimately not doing it for you, then clear the way for something new. If you feel that Rico is someone you can talk to and there are things that can be done to salvage the relationship to grow it into what you need, do that. Just keep things separate so there is no confusion as to why you are doing things. That's my advice."

Ginni had been looking intently at her during this time, soaking in every word. "Is she still coming back?" Ginni smiled nervously.

"Yes, just wrapping up loose ends there and mailing out some boxes of her things. Layce travels light, so there isn't that much."

"Well, thank you for the talk, I really needed it." And she rose from the couch. Jo followed suit. "When will she be back?"

"In a few days."

Just then there was a sound directly above them, a loud thump coming from right over their heads. Immediately, Jo was concerned for her mother. "Mom," she yelled out, as she barreled down the hallway to her bedroom to check if she was in there.

"What, dear," she said as Jo peered into her room, seeing her mother folding her laundry on the bed. Ginni had followed behind her, but stopped short, as to not look into the mother's room out of politeness. She turned to look up the stairs. The dogs began to whine at the steps.

"It came from up there," Ginni said, pointing upstairs.

"I know," Jo said turning around. "It's coming from the cold room." And she looked back over her shoulder to her mother.

Her mother stopped folding the clothes. The dogs ran into the library by the front door wanting no part of whatever it was that made that thud.

"I don't mean to freak you out, Jo, but it sounded to me like a body hitting the ground. It came from right over our head. Is someone up there?"

"No one is up there," Jo said seriously. "I have to go up there," she said almost apologetically. "I have to check it out."

Jo couldn't give in to the trepidation she was feeling. She began climbing the back staircase, with her mother and

Ginni following a few steps behind her. The staircase creaked under their weight, and her sense of dread was increasing. When they arrived at the top of the stairs, they could see that all the doors to the bedrooms had been shut. They always left all the doors but that of the cold room open all the time unless it was bedtime. Jo motioned the women to stay back at the landing, as she moved forward. They obeyed, frightened. The hallway seemed to grow in length as she looked on, and the old-fashioned oil light fixtures were lit dimly. The flicker of the flame was eerie, casting shadows on the wall, and especially since she had not lit them. She looked back at Ginni and her mother, but there was no need to even ask her mother if she lit the hall lights, she knew she didn't.

As she passed Layce's room on the right, she could see her room door was shut as well and slowly, creaking, the cold room door began to open slowly. Jo knew the thud they heard came from that room, and it came from where the closet was. That area was directly over the couches they were sitting in. She looked back at her mother and nodded she would check it out. Her mother looked reluctant to let her go in there, but it had to be done. They moved forward slightly, as Jo began to walk toward the cold room door. The closer she inched her way to the door, the more her body began to feel woozy, as if she were in a dream and floating like a drape in a summer breeze.

In front of her at the end of the hallway in the center just outside the door of the cold room, the dark hall began to manifest what looked like a cloud of smoke slowly materializing in the dimly lit hallway. The concentration of the cloud began to move toward the center and within a few seconds it became a form, but of what? An ungodly sound filled the entire upstairs, yelling out in a deep terrifying rumble, with a distorted white face with black hollow eyes not holding a specific shape, and half the body of the woman in a white dress from the eighteen hundreds, her feet not apparent, screaming out the word 'NO' in a deep boom that sounded nothing like a woman and more like a demon. A giant shadow appeared across the wall like a ghost arm moving up and striking its victim, simultaneously raising Jo up in the air off her feet and throwing her back to where her mother and Ginni were standing on the landing. The door to the cold room slammed shut and began to rattle on its hinges, like a battle was going on in front and behind the door to open or close it.

Ginni and Lorna grabbed Jo's arms quickly and ushered her downstairs and away from the hall and rooms. Jo was frightened and visibly shaken, but she was not injured. Nor did she bear any marks on her body from the slap she had received. The other women were disturbed and confused.

"Oh, my God, Jo, are you okay?" Ginni asked,

panicked, as they set Jo down at the kitchen table. She was trembling.

"What the hell just happened?" Jo asked in a daze and rubbing her elbow and hip that had hit the floor.

"That bitch slapped you. I won't stand for that," Lorna said with contempt, as she began to lose the buzz of the paranormal and anger began to set in. "Nobody hurts my babies." She walked around the kitchen nervously and then began to put the tea on, not knowing what else to do.

"Hand me my phone," Jo said calmly.

Ginni got it off the counter and handed it to her. The only number she could think of to call was Donovan's. He said to call if it happened again. Jo picked up her cell phone and clicked on his number. The phone seemed to load every screen slower than the last. The password, the home screen, the phone icon, the contacts, entering his name in the search bar. Then finally, 'call'. Lorna and Ginni stood quietly in fear and watched Jo, each one taking turns to look up at the stairs, as if some invisible assailant may come after them from above.

"Donovan," she said, her voice having a hint of alarm. "It's happening and its worse this time. I just got thrown down the hall."

There was a pause.

"Yes, I'm okay, but I am a little shaken, obviously. Can you come now?" A few seconds later she put down the phone. "He's coming."

They all waited for Donovan, as the sun went down completely, none of them saying a word; just waiting. The kettle began to whistle on the stove it was ready.

Thirty-One

The doorbell rang. They all jumped out of their seats and followed Jo toward the front door. The dogs were already swarming the door to greet whoever was there, having been hiding out in the library before and after the incident. Jo opened the door to see Donovan's concerned face. "Are you okay?" he said and walked into the house and hugged her.

She was more terrified than she had let on to her mother and Ginni. It had also been a long while since she had felt the embrace of a man and it was comforting. She stood back after the hug and looked at him.

"Donovan, something is happening in this house, and it's centered in that room. I'm scared to go in there right now."

"You said you were thrown?"

"She was, Dr D. We both saw it," Ginni offered and looked at Lorna who nodded her head in agreement.

Donovan seemed to calculate the discussion in his head having no resolution to offer that was rational. Group hysteria was always an option, but he knew Ginni and from what he knew of Jo she was rational, but she had also been under stress.

"Tell me what happened."

They walked back into the kitchen. Lorna and Ginni got tea for everyone, and Jo began to tell him what

182

happened.

"Ginni and I were talking, and we both heard a thud from over our heads. The cold room is over the living room and the thud came from where the closet is. I worried it was my mom, but she was safely in her room downstairs, so I went up and they followed closely behind me. I didn't want them to get hurt — in case of anything," she said shrugging her shoulders, as if to explain why she was the brave one. She was always the responsible one who took risks, the one who protected.

"OK, go on," Donovan said in a serious and inquiring tone.

"OK, first, the dogs wouldn't go upstairs. They were whining and ran into the library. When we went upstairs, all the old-fashioned gas lights were lit in the hall. None of us lit them. Right?" And Jo looked at Lorna and Ginni to confirm. They both nodded in agreement that they hadn't lit them.

"Maybe Layce lit them?" he asked.

"She doesn't know telekinesis," Jo said. He looked at her confused.

"She's in Huntington Beach, packing," Ginni offered.

"Donovan, I saw this with my own eyes. A cloud of smoke or something formed at the end of the hallway, lit with candles that none of us lit ourselves. The smoke made a form that turned into an apparition of a woman in an old white gown but only half of her was showing. The face was scary as shit, Donovan, and she made an ungodly sound and then hit my daughter with some astral slap that knocked her down the hall. We all saw it," Lorna said, worked up as she handed out everyone's teacups. They all took a sip, the three women to calm their nerves, the doctor desperately trying to come up with a rational reason for all of this but struggling too.

"I have to go up there, Jo, and check it out myself," he stated.

"Donovan, I can't be responsible for what happens up there right now. I don't feel safe for you to do that."

"Jo, I have too. There's no other way to handle this."

They all looked at each other and decided he was right. They needed to see what he experienced and if he could help. Jo, although concerned, found her resolve, took a sip of her tea, as if to allow herself one more moment of frailty and then the warrior came over her, as it always had when she was in turmoil. Jo was not the white girl in movies who always fell in front of her attacker, as she was running away. Jo never ran away, and whatever attacked her, she stared in the eyes. She looked head on at her discomforts.

"Okay," she said and stood up. "You guys stay down here." And she and Donovan began walking upstairs. Ginni and Lorna ignored her warning but stayed back slightly, letting them take the lead.

"You two be careful," Lorna cautioned in a motherly tone.

Donovan walked in front of Jo to make sure if any slapping happened this time, it happened to him. When they reached the landing, the three women gasped. All the candle lights were off and all the doors but that of the cold room were closed. The Cold Room door had been shut. Donovan looked at the women. The hallway remained dark, with beams of random light from outside coming in through the window curtains at the end of the hall. Although it was quiet, it was like a false sense of calm, there was a charge in the air that home normally did not have. Like a feeling of electricity that makes your dress cling to your skin, or socks to a shirt out of the laundry.

Donovan and Jo stood on the landing at the top of the stairs and the ladies were high enough on the stairs to see the entirety of the hallway.

"Donovan," Ginni whispered, "those doors were all shut, and the lights were on when we came downstairs. We didn't stop to turn out candles."

They all stared at the hallway. Jo began to get angry inside. She didn't like being played with, nor having something hide its true nature from her when someone else came to see the circus. She took a deep breath and with force said firmly, looking to the end of the hall, "DO IT!"

At once every bedroom door opened bar the cold room, and every candle in the hallway turned on. Something was there, was intelligent and was listening. The

Sufani Weisman-Garza

ladies sucked in air, Ginni covered her mouth in terror. Donovan's head went back slightly, as if taken by surprise.

"I knew you were still here," Jo said sternly to the invisible presence.

Donovan looked on, not knowing what to say, yet stable and with a creased brow. He was trying to understand what was happening but showed no signs of fear. His eyes darted to each door and candle trying to quickly calculate the experience and what to do next.

"Do you believe me now, doctor?" Jo asked in a low voice.

"Yes, ma'am, I do," he said looking around.

"Why do you want me out of that room?" Jo asked the invisible presence, her chest tight with anticipation.

There was a silence and then a high pitched buzz that started low and began to pick up volume. They all covered their ears. It was so loud that they could burst ear drums.

"Enough," Jo yelled out firmly. At once, the buzzing stopped, and the sound was replaced by a child's laughter echoing in the hall. The laughter was not the pleasant kind of child's laughter that makes your heart soar with joy. It was the kind that gave you chills, foreboding and made you not want to turn your back on it. The lights of the candles began flickering and dimmed. Just then there was a shadow, a small shadow slowly making its way down the hall and entered through the door of the cold room. The door had remained shut. Then just like that, the candles turned off on their own and the other doors to the bedrooms remained as they were, open. The static left the air and Jo felt she could breathe again.

"It's over," she said quietly, and looked back at Ginni and her mother. "It's over – for now." Jo motioned to go back.

They all began walking downstairs. "I'm staying the night," Donovan said. All the women shook their heads yes, looking forward.

"We're all sleeping downstairs tonight," Jo said. "There's another bedroom downstairs and the library. Ginni no doubt will shag ass out of here and I will take the room across from Mom. Donovan, you can have the library. It has pocket doors that close and a nice big couch." And she smiled a tired smile. They were all suspended in a sort of disbelief. How could they behave when all that was once believed, stabilized by science, had been proven wrong in front of their eyes? Some truths have the power to cause all security to come plunging down. Their minds filled with spiritual wreckage that had no words to do it justice. Doubts of what reality really was overflowed with a breath-taking silence that pillaged their soul into emptiness. Their group experience, a rare occurrence to have and even stranger among four people at the same time.

"Yes. At this moment, however, I am taking you all out of this house," Donovan said. "Grab your purses and I will take you out for dinner. We need to get out of here for a little while and calm the nerves. I need a moment to think about what happened here and gain my senses again to figure out what we do next."

Not a single one argued. They gathered their things and the dogs hushed, moving like zombies and exited the house, with Jo holding the old-fashioned key to her new haunted house.

Thirty-Two

For a moment upon returning home, they sat in the car looking up at the cold room, not wanting to move out of the car to enter the house again. But they had to.

Jo's phone rang.

"Jo, Layce wants to speak to you," Ginni confessed as they had just made it to the entryway of the house. "I called her. I'm going to go, okay?" she whispered and made her rounds kissing the cheeks of everyone and telling Lorna and Jo to come into the cafe in the morning for breakfast and to talk. They nodded. Jo was relieved to see her go. One less person to get injured.

They had just gotten back from dinner, all much calmer but understanding the house had a mind of its own and therefore was unpredictable. Denial served as a stabilizer, if only momentarily. A luxury never exercised by her. Lorna busied herself getting Donovan set up in the library and the rooms were already made for sleeping comfortably. The heat was on, and the house seemed calm, a calm that couldn't be trusted.

"Hi, Layce. How are you, little sister?" she said with an endearing tone as she took a seat in the living room, happy to be talking about something normal. She moved into the kitchen recounting the story of the night and the hallway incident and, as she suspected, Layce was concerned. She was no stranger to the strange happenings

189

of the house, having had her own incident in the bathroom. Layce assured her she would be home soon, and they would work everything out. Jo was eager for her to come home. Layce was her partner in crime, and they had become even closer since her husband had died, closer still since she had stayed with her. She realized how much Layce was a distraction from her misery and how much she needed her around to help her recover from her ordeal. Layce was good for a laugh and always landed on the lighter side of life, and she needed that. Jo could be funereal enough for the both of them.

After she hung up the phone, she saw that her mother had settled into her room with a cup of hot cocoa and Ginni had long since left the house. She walked to the library to see Donovan getting comfortable on the couch and peeked in. The house was still, but felt alive, as though the velvet wallpaper had eyes and could tell a story of what had transpired in the house over all the years.

"Do you need anything, Donovan?"

He looked up and smiled at her. "Nope, I'm perfect in here surrounded by my favorite things of all time — books."

She smiled back at him and looked around at the laden shelves. "Me too! I'm gonna get you a water though. I'll be right back." And she went to get him a glass of water from the filter in the fridge. "Here you go."

"Oh, thanks," he said, coming forward to receive it

graciously.

"I'm gonna go upstairs to get my pjs on and then I will be down."

His body language got stiff at the idea of her going upstairs. "Do you want me to come with you?"

She laughed a little and said no. She could see he clearly would have dreaded it if she had said yes. "I'm not gonna be afraid of my own house. I know after what happened I should be, Donovan, but maybe it's just sheer stubbornness that keeps me from letting this alter me too much. As of tomorrow, everything is going back to how it was."

"Focusing on the future is good," he said shaking his head. "I think maybe we should do some more research on your property, though, to get a sense of what things have transpired here. It's an old house and must have many stories," he said looking around and even up towards the ceiling. She sensed he was tapping in to the cold room when he made his comment.

She nodded. "I'll go back to see the woman at the historic society. Maybe she found more information. Donovan, you never heard anything not even rumors? Nothing from your mother?"

"No," he said apologetically.

"OK, well, maybe I can see if there are any members of the original family still here in town. That would be something, huh?"

"Yah, that would be something. Listen, go up and get what you need and come right down. Just for tonight, let's give upstairs a rest, and when I say upstairs, I mean us." And he smiled at her. "I'm going to leave the door open here and will listen for you. Just go in your room and no messing about, okay?" His face showed genuine concern and respect for her independence. She was not a damsel in distress, and he respected her moxy. She was formidable in a crisis. He saw that it was not an act, as it was for some of his patients, it was a character trait.

She agreed. She felt the house was different. It felt calm the way it usually was and so she passed her mother's room and began making her way up the back stairs. The dogs left Lorna's room and tagged along with Jo, following her up one stair at a time. She flipped on the electric lights in the stair well for her lighting and made her way up to the landing.

Lorna called out to her. "You're going up?"

All the inhabitants of the house instantly felt a bit on edge for good reason, but neither ran to her to stop her. A little denial was needed to deal with the turmoil they had just gone through and so all were secretly hoping for the best and trying to do mundane things, pretending reality and science were reinstated again as the only truth.

"Yah, just for my pjs. In-n-out. The pups are with me." She took a deep sigh and just walked to her room not even glancing anywhere else, but where she was going. She got her pjs and returned back down the hall, with dogs in tow. They began their descent and passed Lorna on their way into her downstairs room.

"Goodnight, Mother," she said, standing at her door about to shut it and looking in at her mom.

"Goodnight, honey," Lorna said, while laying on her bed, cozy in her bedsocks and legs stretched out on her bed, crossed, looking as comfy as could be. "Everything is gonna be right as rain tomorrow. We'll figure this all out, honey, okay, don't you worry."

Jo smiled. "Yah, it will be fine, Mom. Tomorrow's another day! I'm right here if you need me, okay?"

Lorna nodded her head and kept reading her book.

"Oh, Donovan," Jo yelled out, "I'm going to bed now. Knock on my door if you need anything."

"OK," she heard him yell out from the library.

She put her jams on and folded back the plush sheets and blanket. As she began to think of getting in the bed she looked down and all the dogs were looking up. "I forgot; you guys are so stubby. I have to lift you up, huh?"

They just looked at her and shuffled in place like, Yah, pick us up. You know the drill. She picked each one of them up and placed them on the bed. She crawled in and once she was settled, they took their special place next to her. The events of the day had left her exhausted and so she turned one night stand light off but left the other smaller, dimmer light on. She hit the sheets and was out. Although

Sufani Weisman-Garza

traumatized, the consolation was that the universe allowed them to sleep like the dead.

Sufani Weisman-Garza

Thirty-Three

She felt the soft touch of her hair being stroked and slowly she began to come to, from her sleep. Her eyes peeked out of her slit for eyes, being so sleepy that she felt groggy and it was difficult to bring herself to wake up. She felt as though she had just fallen asleep and now, she was being awakened. She was exhausted, as if she had been out on the town and had been heavily drinking. As her eyes slowly opened, her hair was still tenderly being caressed, she saw the feminine figure of her mother sitting on the edge of the bed and waking her. Jo found it hard to focus her eyes and the room seemed almost dreamlike and cloudy. As her eyes started to focus, up to her neck in lace. She gasped a moment realizing – this was not her mother! It was the woman in white, the one who struck her. Upon her clarity, her body jolted.

"I'm sorry, I'm sorry," the woman said in a voice that could only be explained as hearing someone who was far away with a heavy reverb on their voice. Her inclination was to jump out of bed, but the woman was gentle and apologetic. Was she in a dream? The woman in white continued speaking to her. She seemed paralyzed in her position on the bed but did not feel restrained or scared for that matter. What was happening?

"…(inaudible)…protect (inaudible)…u," she said.

Jo was an observer, struggling to hear the woman's

words and the room was twisting and moving its shape so that she became disoriented. The room was one big cloud. She could see no furniture in the background and only knew herself, as the one looking through her eyes. No dogs, no room, just her looking at the woman and the woman speaking, barely audible.

"The (inaudible)... irl. She's (inaudible) wh... (inaudible) ...Sh... (Inaudible)... eems. You must... (inaudible)."

The look on the woman's face was of concern and Jo felt as though her message was a million miles away. She was communicating, but what was she trying to say? Jo gasped and jerked her body as she awoke from a dream and saw that she was in her guest room bed, the sunlight outside was up and coming in through the drapes and her mother was sitting next to her and stroking her hair just above her ears, just the same way as the woman in her dream was doing. She felt a cold eeriness come over her. It was strange to have a dream of being in bed only to wake to really being in bed. It felt real as though the woman in white was really there and yet her waking reality proved her wrong.

Lorna's eyes got big when she saw Jo's jumpy reaction and said, "It's okay, hun, it's just me. It's time to wake up. It's 11 o'clock already."

"What?" Jo said rubbing her eyes in disbelief that she had slept so long. "Mom, I had a weird dream."

Just as she said that, Ginni and Layce peeked their heads into the room. Jo sat up in bed. "You're home already? How?" she asked Layce, as Layce and Ginni approached the side of her bed.

"After our call, I changed my flight. I got all my stuff packed in the storage pod and it's on its way. Ginni picked me up and here I am. I couldn't let you be home another day here without me. It didn't feel right not being here with you."

Jo was touched by that and grabbed Layce's hand gently to touch it. She truly appreciated her sister being there. She was pure sunshine and just having her in the house made a difference to her spirit. "Awe, I appreciate that, Layce. Thanks, Sis." Jo felt genuine relief.

Layce leaned in and hugged her.

"I had the weirdest dream. The lady in white was caressing my hair and I think she was apologizing. Yes, she was stroking my hair and saying I'm sorry. She was telling me a message, but it was choppy."

The girls had sat at the end of the bed. The dogs had clearly been up early and out of the room doing their own things because they no longer occupied the bed.

"What did she say, Jo?" her mother asked. They were very interested, having all had an interaction with the woman in white.

"I couldn't make most of it out, it was too far away sounding and so echoic. But the word I did get was,

'protect'. I think she hit me to keep me out of that room."
Jo looked around at the women intently, pondering her finding. "I think she is here trying to protect us."

This was a new revelation. They were all quiet, trying to sort it out in their own minds.

"Jo, she hit you," Ginni commented, seeing the strike at her to be dangerous, not protective.

"Yes, but she didn't hurt me. Her motivation could have been to get me away from the door. And, Layce, when you were in the bathroom, there was more than one entity in that bathroom and the one that came out of the tiles didn't harm you. It was the woman in white, right? You said you could see the white collar on her neck? But she seemed to be having an interaction with the entity in front of you, right?"

Layce looked at Ginni and then her mother nodding her head at the possibility. "It's possible. Still, we need to be careful Jo."

"You need to get someone in here, Jo, to clean the place up. Do a little Gris-Gris," Ginni said.

"Vodou? Oh man!" she said distraught. "Do you really think we need that? I know it's a beautiful religion, but I'm not really into any religion. But I like that one a lot more than most," she said getting out of bed. "It's misunderstood."

"Isn't Voodoo bad?" Lorna asked confused and concerned.

"No, Mom, not really. All the bad things you have heard is a bunch of bullshit Hollywood crap. I mean, it's just like any other religion. People can distort what is good, but it isn't the way you see it in movies. It's actually full of ritual and sacred worship. Clay's cousin is a Mambo. I haven't talked to any of the family for a while," she said with a solemn tone, as if a fresh memory had just entered her mind.

"What's a Mambo?" Layce asked.

"It's like a woman priest," Ginni answered her.

"How do you know this stuff, Ginni?" Jo asked, then they both answered at the same time.

"N'Awlins." And smiled.

"I thought so. You learned Voodoo. Clay's family is from the original V-o-d-o-u birthplace, Benin, Africa. We only went out there once. I met the family, but I didn't know the cousins well, just his mom and sister. I can call Adama," she looked at Ginni, "that's Clay's sister, to see what she suggests. I should call them anyway," she said going into a momentary deep thought for Clay, with a sudden and quick sadness coming over her face. "In the meantime, I'm gonna get ready and pay Miss Geraldine from the Historical society another visit and see if she found anything else on the house and perhaps if any of the Purdys who built this house still live in this area. Wouldn't that be something?" she said, looking at her mother and then Layce. "If anyone knows anything about this house, it would be embedded in their family stories somewhere, right?"

"That's a long shot Sis. Just sayin'. It's possible though – just don't get your hopes up too much for the original family to still be in town."

"I know. Hey, did Donovan leave?" she inquired.

"Oh, yes. He's gone, dear. Early this morning. Said he had to go home and shower for work. I packed him a lunch," and she smiled a cute flirty smile. "He's a cutie pie, for sure." And she giggled.

Jo laughed silently at her mother and how cute she was. "Now, anything new occur that I need to know?"

"No, dear. It's been silent, and the house feels good. No strange weather in the house," Lorna replied. She used to always call negative feelings or bad energy in a house from fighting and such, 'bad or strange weather in the house'. It was cute.

"Okay, well, I'm gonna go get ready."

"In your room?" Layce asked.

"Yes."

"Ginni and I will sit in your room while you shower, you know, just to be there, okay, Sis. I will feel better being there with you for now. I don't trust these bathrooms," she said referring to her terrifying experience.

"Okay, thank you." They walked out of the room and Lorna had gotten her a cup of hot coffee to take upstairs with her.

"Thanks, Mom."

Nos, Ferrah, and Tu came running out of the library to see her and she gave them a few pats. "You guys want to come up stairs with us?" They at once began making the trek up the stairs in their ridiculous style of huffing and puffing, fighting to get their big bodies and short legs up the staircase. You could hear the sound of snorting, feet running in the hall, doggie nails scratching the hardwood and then onto the carpet once they hit the landing and took off to her room. Seeing the initial view of the hall and the walk through it to get to her room initially gave her an undercurrent of fear. She felt a twinge of unease, but she sensed at the moment the weather in the house was calm, and so she brushed off the feeling and headed down the hall and into her room. They all went with Jo except Lorna, who stayed downstairs knitting and singing songs quietly in the living room, looking out the front window occasionally, as she rocked on one of the old fashioned rockers. She sang some sort of ancient lullaby, as she rocked. Although Lorna was an older woman, she was a bad ass in her own right and would fight to the death for her children. She was a mother you wanted around when the shit hit the fan. She was as sturdy and grounded as a rock, sharp as a whip and yet pulled off a sweet grandma persona. She was genuine, and all her good qualities rubbed off on her girls; the girls who were now in danger from something unseen in the house. She quietly rocked, occasionally looking out in reticence. But was her peaceful disposition really just her primal engine quietly firing under a veil of protective thought? Lorna always got quiet before a battle to protect her children. She did not scare easy. It's where Jo got it from.

Thirty-Four

It was after twelve when Jo was ready to head out to the historical society to see Geraldine. She had never called with any other information, yet she had more requests to ask of Geraldine. Perhaps she would know if some of the original homeowner's family still lived in Gig Harbor?

The thought lingered in her mind about calling Clay's family, but she just couldn't do it yet. She wasn't ready. It was too close to the nerve still and she was just beginning to feel like she could move on. Bringing his family in right now and in this capacity was just too much stress for her. Someone neutral to her would feel more comfortable. She just felt that she could let her pain and emotions out in little bits and that made her feel as though she were dealing with the pain from her loss on her own terms in small manageable bites. To contact her extended family would peel the lid off completely and she just wasn't willing to do that. The thought of it all gave her anxiety, as it did when she lived in her old hometown and the reason she needed to move away. It was working for her, and she needed to keep that going to really heal over time. She felt Gig Harbor's healing balm on her spirit and the nice way in which people accepted her. It was quaint and a little slower than what she was used to. It was what the doctor ordered.

"Are you guys ready to go?" Jo called out as she

203

walked down the stairs. She could hear them in the kitchen giggling and having a good time. It sounded like the healthy banter of new love, a momentary lapse of memory of the house's horrors. She entered the kitchen to see them face to face, standing in front of the coffee pots and loosely holding each other's hands on the verge of a kiss, or secret.

"Oh boy, you two are too cute," Jo announced as she stopped to look at the budding new love and smiled. "Does this mean you guys are doing the grownup now?" Jo laughed to herself and moved on to pick up her purse and throw it around her shoulder.

"Jo!" Layce yelled at her playfully and with a tone of correction.

"Oh, relax, Layce," Ginni replied. "She's just being real. No, to answer your question; Layce has performance anxiety," she told her and started to laugh. Layce also burst out in laughter.

"Oh, is that what 'going slow' is called these days?" Layce asked. "Just 'cause you're whorey doesn't mean I have performance anxiety."

The coffee in Ginni's throat almost came out her nose from the shock and hilarity of what Layce had said. They were new and had not yet learned the rhythms of each other's speech. Were they all in denial, acting as though nothing happened the night before? They all walked to the door and Jo yelled out to Lorna they were going to the Historical Society for a little bit and would be back.

Sufani Weisman-Garza

"Are you sure you don't want to come, Mom?" Jo yelled out from the front door, turning her ear to hear the reply while looking down the long hallway and the front staircase leading upstairs. She was feeling uncomfortable with leaving Lorna in the house. The house felt unpredictable bordering on dangerous at times and until things were understood and 'handled' she didn't feel good about leaving the house.

"Yes, honey. I want to knit and call my boyfriend. I'll finally have the house alone so we can have phone sex if we want to." And she peeked her head out of her bedroom smirking and saw them all laughing.

"Lorna, you are so adorable," Ginni said smiling at her.

Jo's smile soon faded, "OK, Mom," she said with trepidation. "Call if you need us or anything on the way home. Love you."

"Love you too, girls." And she went back into her room.

The house grew silent.

The girls all left the house and the dogs. The dogs walked to Lorna's room to hang out with her for a while. Lorna had bigger plans in the house than she led on. When she heard the door shut completely and lock, she put down her knitting needles and got up from her chair and headed up the stairs. The dogs whined and wouldn't go after her. Phone sex was not her mission after all.

Thirty-Five

Jo, Ginni and Layce were all in the car on their way to the historical records building.

"All right you two, what's up with you? Ginni, did you break up with Rico yet, or what?"

"Not yet," Ginni answered. "I'm going over to his place tomorrow to talk to him about it."

Layce made a look of disapproval but said nothing. Jo ignored her facial expression. "That's good, Ginni. Don't wait. You don't want people seeing you around with Layce and him finds out that way. Just rip off the Band-Aid and let him know. It is more compassionate than letting him think it's him."

Ginni agreed and they said nothing more on that matter.

They drove for fifteen minutes and arrived at the records building. When they all went inside, they let Jo take the lead.

Geraldine recognized Jo and smiled as she walked over. "And today we've brought an entourage, I see," Geraldine said cheerfully. "Oh, hello, Ginni. How are you?" And she reached out her hand.

"Nice to see you too, Geraldine. Haven't seen you at Mamma's Cafe for a while?"

"Trying to watch my girlish figure. Can't stay sexy eating big breakfasts all the time," she said moving her shoulders and hips like Mae West.

They all giggled.

"This is my sister, Layce," Jo said pointing to Layce who had not yet been introduced.

Geraldine stepped forward tilting her head with a smile. "This is the beloved little sister, I see." And she smiled at Jo and then back at Layce. "Well, it is a pleasure to meet the family and now we all know one another. How friendly of us!" she said playfully and moved on to business. "So, what has brought all of you here today; what can I do?"

"Well, I was wondering first if you had learned anything else about the house history, and secondly if there are any original descendants from the Purdy family, the original builders of the home?" Jo said, turning to the girls to explain who the Purdys were, and then back to Geraldine.

"Oh, I see, so, small stuff?" she said laughing to herself and began walking to the back round table, waving them all to come, and sit. They followed closely behind her. She sat and they all took a seat. "You are in luck, Jo, an original Purdy family member is still in town. Her name is Nina Levensven. It's strange but I was doing work on your file and a woman came in to look in for building records of a property her company is interested in buying, and it is their custom to check out the records. She saw the file I had out of your home and asked about it. She seemed intrigued. I simply told her the new homeowner was doing some research and she revealed to me her family used to live in that home. The more I spoke to her, the more I learned that her family were actually the original homeowners. She is somehow connected through the mother's lineage. I believe she told me through the mother's sister's side. Isn't that fascinating how things happen like that? She could have come on any other day when the file would not have been out, and I would have never known. It's almost like the house wanted you to know," she said and smiled a look of kismet.

"Oh, that's wonderful. May we have her number or …" and as Jo was speaking, Geraldine handed her a card with Nina's name on it. Jo stopped speaking and took the card in silence studying it. "Thank you," she said. "Did she say anything when she gave this to you for me?"

"Yes. She inquired how long you had been there, and then said that by now you surely had some questions, somewhat mysteriously and facetiously. Then she went to her own business and left."

"Oh."

"Johannah?" Geraldine said in a pondering, questioning tone. "She is a bit strange. I wanted you to know."

The girls all looked at each other.

"Something else happen in the house, Jo?" Geraldine asked inquisitively.

"The house has become alive, Geraldine. It's become

a little hot tempered and unpredictable there. Scary at times, but not always. It's strange," Jo said, with confusion. "At times, I am absolutely at home and feel comforted by the house. Then other times I feel like the house is plotting something, the energy become intense and puts everyone on edge."

"Yes, and don't forget to tell her that it is truly paranormal," Layce offered and looked at Jo and then at Geraldine again. "It threw her across the hallway the other night. That's why we must know more about the house."

"Oh dear, that's concerning, Jo. Are you okay?" she said suddenly feeling her safety was at risk.

"Yes, but a little shaken up of course. Not sure how to proceed."

"Oh, yes, Nina did say one more thing that I just remembered. I didn't understand it then but now it makes more sense. She said, 'Only certain people know how to handle that house.' Maybe she meant people to cleanse it, or something of that nature. What do you think?"

"Hmm, that is interesting. But you never had the owners before me come to you with any similar stories, right?"

"No, I never met them. But they lived in that house a very long time and I have only been here for not quite ten years. The woman before me may have spoken with them on similar accounts. It's hard to know."

"Perhaps I could speak with the woman before you?"

Jo asked.

"Impossible, I'm afraid. She passed away," Geraldine said and shook her head sadly. "She was a nice woman. I took her place when she passed on. I knew her from around town, but not well. Just that she was a nice woman."

"OK, well, I'll give Nina a call and see what she meant. On the other matter, did you find anything additional on the house itself for me?"

"No, dear, nothing has come up in my search regarding any personal history. Families do tend to keep information close to the chest if you know what I mean?" she said leaning in and lowering her voice as if telling Jo a secret. "Of course, I will continue to look into it. If I can catch Nina around town I will inquire and snoop a little," she said smiling facetiously. "However, I did want to talk to you about something. The society has done extensive work on getting your house onto the national historic registry already. Maybe we could talk about finalizing that when you are ready?"

"Oh, really? Wow, that's,...unexpected," Jo said, "but also wonderful."

Geraldine smiled. In a nutshell, the society is tasked with finding buildings and locations that have historical significance to the town. Your house is one. There are a few things that would still need your involvement to finalize it, and it is quite involved. With all you're going through right now, I wouldn't want to add any more stress to your life, and I must tell you, it can be a little daunting, processes, that sort of thing."

"Oh, Geraldine. It sounds like something I absolutely would love to do, but the timing…I need a little time to recover before starting a project, if you don't mind?'

"Of course, dear. It's all up to you. Anyone can nominate a house for historical registry, and the society can gather all the historical data, as we have done on the building, materials, that sort of thing, but only the owner can choose to put it in the national registry for all to see."

"Oh, I see," Jo said considering it all.

"It might be a bit much for you right now, Jo," Layce said.

"I have to agree with Layce, Jo. Now doesn't seem like the right time, but the right time will come!" Geraldine said. "There's no hurry at all, Jo. You let me know when you're ready."

Geraldine was the most kind and understanding woman.

"Thank you for understanding Geraldine."

"Of course deary. Anyhoosie, families don't like to spread their dirty laundry out to the public, and they certainly do all they can to keep their family business out of the papers or from being logged in historical records. Nina seemed the best bet. She would start there.

"OK, Geraldine, well as usual, you were amazing and

I had a great time with you," Jo said shaking her hand warmly, with her other hand on top of Geraldine's.

Geraldine smiled at her. "And nice meeting you, ladies," she said to Layce and Ginni.

They said their farewells and were out the door and back in the car.

"Someone please call Mom and tell her we're on our way home. I don't want to walk in on phone sex," Jo said and laughed.

Layce smiled and punched in her mother's number. After a few seconds, Jo looked at Layce from the rear-view mirror, and Ginni was looking back at Layce.

"She isn't answering, and she isn't on the other line," Layce said concerned, body language stiffened, and alarm resonated through their silence.

The urgency to get home went from one to ten and the silence in the car became a group fear that something had happened to their mother. Jo picked up speed and none of them said a word, all looking forward and deep in thought.

Thirty-Six

Lorna was a light-hearted, stubborn, rogue rule breaker and always had been. The minute the girls were out the door she had a mind to go up into the cold room. As she reached the landing at the top of the staircase, she looked at the hall and it showed no air of intrigue. Still, she approached cautiously. A feeling was present in the hallway, perhaps it was her own tension and fear, as she walked forward? When she got closer to the cold room and the door opened on its own, inviting her in, she knew it was more than her own energy she sensed. Whatever was in that room wanted her to go in. She took a cautious breath and stepped in. Feeling the chill, she hugged herself in an attempt to warm up. Although the muted sun came through the room, it still had the air of seclusion and dark shadows, the farther back and toward the closet the room went. She looked toward the windows and saw the trees and then turned toward the closet; as the closet door in front of her began to open slowly on its own, letting out a darkness that was darker than the shadows, the door behind her creaked shut. She stepped closer, intending to investigate what was inside, despite her immediate fear. As she approached the closet, she glanced back at the trees outside, as though she may not see them again. She became filled with instant regret at her decision to enter the room alone, with no backup.

213

Thirty-Seven

"What if she's just talking to her boyfriend or something?" Ginni said, as they all stood in front of the house at the front stair looking up at the room. "She could just be busy, and we're getting all worked up for nothing."

Jo shushed them with her hand to stop bickering and went up the front stairs to the porch with the girls following her.

She put the key in, and the door did not open. "God damn it," Jo yelled out in frustration. "Open this fucking door!" And the lock clicked. She may as well have said open sesame. The door was open.

"Thank you, Ali Baba," Layce whispered, and they all piled into the house. The dogs were not at the door. The library door was closed, and Jo motioned for Ginni to open it, as they walked forward. The dogs were on the couch and Tu was on the floor at the couch. They didn't move. It was odd.

The house was eerily silent with the stillness of static in the air and the familiar feeling that something was not right in the house. They all knew what it meant.

"Mom!" Jo yelled out.

No answer.

"Mom!" Layce called.

No answer.

There was a thump on the ceiling of the living room

214

to their right. It could come from no other than the cold room. Jo's feeling of dread came over her body like an internal hot flash, knowing that her mother was in there. Why was her mother in there?

"Oh my God!" Jo ran up the front staircase that was rarely used, just past the library. That staircase landed them in the middle of the hallway upstairs and she ran toward the cold room. The door was closed. She twisted the doorknob and the room that had no lock would not open. She kicked it and slammed her body into the door.

"Mom," Jo yelled at the door pounding on it and yelling again. The slapping of her open hand on the door stung her palm and she began pounding it with her fist and shoving her shoulder into the door to make it open. Her efforts met with resistance.

A dark mist began to form to her right where the end of the hallway window was, just as before. For a moment, she stood back away from the door turning to the right to see the mist growing and forming into a shape. Jo waited a few seconds backing away from the door slightly, thinking over what to do. But she wasn't about to wait while her mother could be in there.

"Not today, woman," Jo said to the forming mist not caring if she was hit, slapped or thrown again..

"It's happening again," Ginni said, terrified.

"Fuck it," Jo said kicking the door hard and watching it slam open. What they saw brought no comfort, but terror beyond what they had ever known. Lorna was suspended over the bed unconscious while items in the room flew about the air suspended by a fierce gust of wind whipping things out around even though every door and window was shut.

The moment that Jo stepped into the room, she looked at the closet. It was open. It was as though the closet saw she was back and shut its door immediately. At that same moment, everything, including Lorna, dropped from its spell. Lorna crashed down onto the bed, waking her from her repose. The howl of the wind ceased and the sound of items crashing on the floor and breaking peaked; then there was silence. When Lorna hit the bed, her eyes bolted open, as though she were released from a forced conformity.

"What happened?" Lorna yelled out and got off the bed quickly straightening her pencil skirt and sweater blouse.

Ginni and Layce stood terrified at the door, eyes bulging.

Before any more words were said, Jo took her mother by the arm and ushered her out of the room and closed the door. Jo was not only horrified, but angry. This was an attack on her mother that she was not going to stand for.

"*Why did you go in there?*" she said to her mother, shaking her.

Sufani Weisman-Garza

Layce opened the door to Jo's room, and they all stepped inside and closed the door tightly. Jo's room had become something of a safe room. But terror layout side Jo's door and they had just scratched the surface of what the house could do. Lorna sat down on the bed, shaken; her hair that was pulled up earlier was windblown and messy. She needed a minute to speak and settle her nerves. Jo kneeled down in front of her, and Layce sat next to her mother on the bed. Ginni remained standing, securing a foot at the door, just to be safe.

"Mom, tell me what happened," Jo asked, not sure she was ready for what her mother would tell her. Her mother paused and then began to speak.

Thirty-Eight

"I don't know what happened, Jo. I remember," she said contemplating, "I went in there to communicate with the room. I don't like that the room is somehow controlling you and everyone in this house," she said adamantly. "The door opened easily for me and seemed quiet and at peace when I entered. It was chilly, as it normally is. The rest…I don't remember a thing Jo," she said perplexed. "I just remember waking up on the bed and the terrified looks on your faces. That and this feeling I have, as though I somehow had my soul stolen, for however long I was in that room."

"When did you go into that room?" Jo asked.

"As soon as you left." The girls all looked at one another. They had been gone for over an hour and she remembered nothing.

"OK, well, this is getting too dangerous," Jo said getting up from the floor pacing and holding her chin. She looked out at the trees through her bay window pondering a decision. "You need to go home, Mom, until we get this settled. I can't have anything happen to you in this house or have you under stress. And, Layce, I will totally understand if you want to change your mind and not live here. I will help you move into your own apartment until I get this handled."

"No way, Jo!" Layce shouted out. "I'm not leaving you

here in this Frankenstein house."

Jo sighed hard, grateful to not be left alone there.

Lorna knew it was best for her not to be under that stress at her age and stage in her life and did not put up a fight. Jo sat next to her on the bed.

"Mom, I will get this stuff settled and then you can come back out to the house when it's safer for you. In the meantime, when you come out, I will get you a little apartment, cottage, guest house or hotel, depending on how long you want to stay. Okay?"

Lorna agreed, still visibly shaken.

They opened Jo's door, and all went downstairs, each cautiously eyeing the door of the cold room as they passed, barricading Lorna from the door as they went by.

After a few phone calls, and hours later, Lorna's bags were packed, she was taken out to lunch and was on an airplane heading home to the safety of her own house and boyfriend. This was too close a call with her mother and if anything had happened to her, Jo would not be able to forgive herself.

When they all got home after stalling for some time at Mamma's Cafe drinking coffee and eating pastries, Jo stood in the kitchen as the girls were in the living room watching TV with the dogs and she dug into her purse to phone the woman whose family used to own her home. Thirty minutes later, there was a knock on the door.

"Nina Levensven?" Jo asked to the woman standing

on her porch. She had straight black hair cut in a bob, pale skin, and rouged lips. She was dressed professionally in all black; a tight skirt just below her knees and a double breasted fitted matching suit jacket with four-inch stiletto heels. Her appearance was beautiful – beautiful and cold.

"You should have never moved in here," she said, her piercing ice blue eyes staring at Jo and then without asking walked into the home and closed the open door, as if to keep a secret behind the two front doors. Jo moved out of the way for her entry. Intrigued by her, Jo knew she knew more about the house than what was on paper and was feeling afraid of what she was about to find out. Once she knew the story, she could not un-know it.

Nina Levenson walked directly into the living room where Ginni and Layce were watching TV, and the dogs lay at the floor of the couch at their feet. The dogs made no sound or effort to approach her. Even the air seemed to hold its breath. She walked in front of the TV, oblivious to all of them in the living room, and looked up at the ceiling. Jo felt a chill. This woman was a sensitive, but what side she worked for could not immediately be discerned. Her energy felt cloaked in menace and iciness.

"Jesus! They're all still here," she said lowering her head from the ceiling and looking at Jo. "How many have you seen?"

Jo looked shocked. "How many are there?"

Nina laughed and walked toward her licking her lips.

"That's a good question," she said getting close to Jo and smirking. "We only know for sure about the ones that were murdered and found. It's the ones that weren't found…" she said and lingered off toward the front staircase, looking upstairs, while holding the banister. Her thoughts seemed to trail off into deep waters. "Can't you feel them in the house?" she asked rhetorically. She turned to Jo. "Of course, you can. That's why you called." Her demeanor seemed to change from an eerie magical darkness to a more business facade.

"What do you mean 'the ones who were murdered and found'?" Jo asked, as they all looked at Nina for the answer.

The conversation was chilly and frightening.

"You don't know there were three brutal murders confirmed in this house?" she said walking around the foyer and peeking in rooms. "You did a very nice job with the place. It is a magnificent house."

Jo felt her body get hot and it felt as though her heart stopped beating, and beads of sweat began to form on her upper lip and forehead. Layce rose at the sight of her sister's distress and came to be by her. This was the worst possible news she could hear.

"What happened?" Jo demanded.

"Well, the story has it," she said walking toward the door, as though she were ready to leave, "that the Purdy parents were not such great parents. They had a small daughter, who they killed, so the story goes," she said nonchalantly. "The legend in my family is that the little girl fought back and delivered some blows to the parents that ultimately killed them after she was murdered by her parents."

"Why would they do that?" Jo asked traumatized by every word out of Nina's mouth, one story worse than the next, and Nina seeming to take some perverse pleasure at dropping a psychological bomb in her life.

"Who knows?" she said flippantly. "It was surprising though. The Purdys were always known for spoiling their daughter and giving her lots of toys and dolls. They were known in town later to have been linked to missing children in town at that time too, and legend has it that that they may have even been serial killers. The children were never found." And she twisted the door and opened it and stepped onto the porch.

"How many children?" Jo asked.

"At least a dozen," Nina said whimsically, as though discussing Easter eggs. "As beautiful as this place is, it still gives me the creeps, even after all these years," she said scoping the house. "Why did you come here?" Referring to Gig Harbor as a place she was bored with. "And why this house?" As she stepped down the steps to leave. "Let me guess," she said turning her head back at Jo, as she descended to the bottom stair while holding the railing, "you had a death trauma too that brought you here?" And she smiled as though she was pleased with herself. How did she know about Jo's husband's suicide? And was it some pattern?

Jo was silent and felt the frigidity of this woman's soul, and Layce and Ginni stood next to her at the door supporting her, the dogs at their feet.

"The house is talking to you," Nina said, and she looked up at the cold room and pointed her finger three times at the window. "And you better listen!" She got into her black sleek Mercedes sedan and drove off.

Jo was happy to see her go and frozen in her words. The girls stood for a few extra seconds at the front door letting her words sink in while taking in the nightfall air. Jo shut the door that kept the house secrets in all these years. She had met three of the spirits. Serial killers, kept repeating in her head. Were there more dead in the house, and were they upstairs in the cold room? Was the woman in the white dress trying to keep them out for their shame of horror for what they had done to their daughter and possibly others? Children? The thought was too much to bear. How could anyone hurt a child?

Thirty-Nine

The next morning Jo and Layce went to Mamma's Cafe. They were tired from the events of the house and the stress it entailed. Jo was filled with determination to resolve the issues in the house once and for all. Ginni worked behind the counter but tended to Jo and the woman she was now seeing. Rico had been told about Ginni's relationship with Layce and he was very upset according to Ginni. But all was fair in love and war and life went on. It would be awkward when they ran into one another, but that was a small price to pay for love's sake.

"So, what I want to do," Jo started to say as Ginni stood at their table pouring coffee, "is make the guest house out in back into an apartment. It is separated from the house and hopefully clear of all tension inside the home. They wouldn't have been out in the guest house. It would have been used for servants. Things were much different in those times. Class would have kept them from entering the servants' quarters. Things are in decent order there. I will enlist some help from the movers who helped me in the beginning to help move some things around and put things in storage. There is an attic in the guest house where we can move some of these items in the guest house too. We'll stay in there to sleep until we get this shit in order." She referred to the ghost problem in the house like a bug infestation. "We need to be well rested, and I

224

don't feel comfortable in my own house to sleep."

Ginni and Layce shook their heads in lament.

"Layce, we'll get started when we get back to the house okay? We'll be in there tonight. This is a one-day gig."

"OK, I feel better about that for now. But what are we gonna do? You can't give up your house and live like a refugee in the guest house," Layce commented.

"No, I don't intend to. In dealing with fear, Layce, the only way out, is in."

"You're gonna go in there yourself?"

"There's no other way, Layce. And I don't care what tries to prevent me. I am going to figure out what is going on in that room. I just don't feel right surrendering to whatever is in my house. It's speaking to me, like Nina said, and I am gonna listen. And not only listen, but I'm also gonna ask questions. I just don't understand something." And Jo looked perplexed while she took a sip of coffee and picked a piece off a crumb cake from the plate in front of her. "I don't understand the parents. I saw the man, the father, my first night – remember? And the mother hit me and pushed me away from the door, which in itself seemed violent. But in my dreams when she came to me, she was gentle and was like a mother figure protecting me."

"Yes, and when I saw the girl in the bathroom when I took a bath," Layce said, "it seemed like the woman in white was blocking me from the girl, not the other way around. It was all freaky, but if I look at it and how I felt about each entity when it was happening, I felt something sinister from the girl, not the woman in white. I think the girl is in that closet. Something feels wrong about her, Jo, something we need to be afraid of. We've seen what she did to Mom. Who knows what else she can do?"

"But we don't know it was her doing those things. There are three in the house that we know of. Travesties have occurred in this house?" Jo said, questioning its history. "Whatever the truth is, it needs to be uncovered before there can be peace. That I know!"

"Peace restores many things, sister,' Layce said, and she touched Jo's hand. It had not gone unnoticed by Layce that the glacial woman, Nina, had brought up the tragedy of Clay's suicide, as a reason that she was drawn to the house.

"I have to get back to work, you guys. I'm here all day so I won't be much help to you. How about I bring you dinner tonight after work? You'll be hungry and not in the mood to
cook," Ginni offered.

"That sounds great," Layce said and Ginni leaned over and kissed her and went back to work. Jo smiled at their new budding love.

"You guys are too cute."

"Thanks, Sis. Look, about what Nina said about being drawn to the house?" Layce said.

"I think it's true," Jo said. "Something in the energy of what I have been through drew me into this house. And, why am I having this experience here when others have lived here and never had a problem?."

"Well, you don't know, though, if they had no experience. You just know nothing was reported. It seems to have been a well-kept secret in the family lineage and history of the house that not even Geraldine had anything documented on, or knowledge of. Why was there nothing printed? She said the town suspected them. Surely, they would have been tried by the press of the time?"

"You know, Geraldine also said she took over for someone who knew a lot more than her. If she wasn't born here, she wouldn't know the lore of the county. These things seem to be embedded in the history and quietly kept hidden within families, except for people who stumble upon it by accident, or circumstance. Maybe you were just chosen to help release these spirits from the house, Sis?"

"Maybe, but I don't want to be 'the One'," she said, knowing that despite her wants, she would have to do the work. "I remember some things about clearing homes and I will do it. I must go into that closet though. I think the girl is in that closet. I need to see what's in that little area in the floor, remember?" She spoke with trepidation.

"Òh, yah! There was a loose piece of the floor you were pulling up when the door closed on us that time. Other than that, though, it just looked like a normal closet.

I mean, not normal, huge, but a closet with hangers and poles."

"Yes, but that closet suspends things in the air, opens and closes itself and locks people in and out with no locks. There is something to that area. It's almost as though the room door, and then the room itself, are barriers, or gates blocking the closet. I got the feeling that when we were in the closet, we were the ones being inspected. Didn't you, looking back?"

Layce nodded her head. "Jo, I'm scared to go back in there."

"I know. But you better work your fear out and think like a warrior, Layce. When we go in there, we are on a mission to uncover what lies beneath. Fear is a weakness we can't afford to have. You can be scared now, but the day we go in, your mind needs to be like a soldier. Mine too. It's the only way to keep our heads."

"Okay," Layce said, and they continued with breakfast and then off to the house to get the guest house ready.

Later in the afternoon, movers came to help and move large pieces of furniture and boxes from the rooms and into the attic. Jo had leftover items from her storage in there, and so with the help of Layce and the movers she had made the two-bedroom guest house a very comfortable apartment for them to live in for the time being.

By nightfall, they were comfortable in the apartment

with the dogs and Ginni had come bearing dinner as she promised. Tomorrow was another day. Tomorrow was the day she would go back into the house to clear it from negativity and to attempt to clear the bedroom and what was inside that closet.

Forty

Morning came and Jo was awakened by the singing of birds in the tree that hung over the cottage. There was morning sunlight beaming through the grey and for the time being the birds were celebrating. The sunlight and song betrayed her true feelings of foreboding. That sun in the wintertime often did not last the whole day and sometimes it was only momentary. Nevertheless, the birds rejoiced by singing songs of celebration. The heaviness in her spirit reminded her of her job ahead. The dogs were cuddled up with her and lifted their heads when she lifted hers. She pet them and said hello with a promise to feed them and take them out for a walk.

The harbor created crispness to the air that was bone chilling at times and made Jo want to stay in bed. Sometimes it wasn't the only thing that made her want to stay in bed. But the cold also made tea and coffee that much better. She smelled a brew in the air and knew that Layce must be awake. They had made sure the day before to bring in the necessities in order to have what they needed in the morning before they got busy.

She climbed out of bed and the dogs with her. She put on her jeans and sweater. She had showered the night before, so she was ready to go with a few touch ups. She fed the dogs first, and then took them for a walk around the block while the sun was still out and it wasn't raining.

230

As she entered back into the cottage the dogs were noisy snorting and shaking their collars and happy to be back inside where it was warm. Now tea and scones for her. Entering the kitchen, she found Layce and Ginni in the kitchen chattering away and they quickly gave the dogs some love. Jo was surprised, not expecting to see Ginni so early. The servants' quarters were quant with all the touches of a Victorian, only slightly subdued from that of the house. Servants did not get stained glass windows or crystal doorknobs.

"Oh, good morning," she said, as Layce turned and handed her a cup of coffee and smiled.

"Good morning," they said in unison and smiled at each other. What was it about calamity that brought people together? She felt the same dis-ease of another 'event' bringing people together in expectation – the feeling uncomfortable as it always was, and the reason she moved away. Perhaps no one can run away from themselves after all?

"Oh, I picked these up for you guys. They're new at the cafe. So cute! Called 'Scone Henge'," Ginni said handing the plate she had prepared for them. They looked like biscuits. "These are mixed berry. They're organic and gluten free."

Jo took the plate and sat down. "Cute! Thanks, Ginni. Are you staying while we start cleansing the house?"

"No, I'm just leaving now actually to work. But I am gonna have my phone on and if there is anything that happens, call me. I'm just down the street. Please be careful!" she said with a look of concern and kissed Layce, said goodbye to Jo and was out the door. Ginni clearly was not a fan of the macabre and couldn't leave fast enough. A blanket of grey crossed over the one beam of sun that was struggling to exist. The air got colder.

"How are you feeling about this, Layce?" Jo needed to know her feelings about the attempt they were about to make to rid the house of its unwanted guests and experiences as a result.

"Nervous, of course, but ready to claim your house," she said. "How are you feeling about it?"

"I'm feeling like anything can happen. I have this feeling like something could happen in the house today. The vibe feels unstable. I guess I'm nervous," she said exhausted. "Just listen to me, okay, Layce? Whatever I say to you, do, alright?"

Lacy shook her head yes, taking her question seriously and agreeing. "What's the plan?"

Jo said nothing, she just got up and went into the room she had slept in, and Layce followed. She went up into the closet digging for something specific and pulled out a medium-sized box with a lock latch and two handles. It was heavy as she carefully brought it down from the shelf making sure that she did not also move other items that were stacked there. She held it in silence and Layce instinctively knew not to speak, as Jo maneuvered the box on to the bed. Once she placed it down, she looked at it like an old friend and took in a deep breath, letting out a great sigh.

"What is it, Jo?" Layce asked, hushed by the feeling in the room. Jo was quiet for a moment.

"It's from Benin," she said in a whisper, focused on the box. "It's something Clay taught me, and ceremonies I was part of when I went to Benin with him." And she ran her fingers over the box. Gathering it closer she grabbed her keys and asked Layce if she was ready to go inside the big house.

Layce reluctantly nodded her head and they left the guest cottage with keys and the mysterious box in hand.

Sufani Weisman-Garza

Forty-One

The key opened the back door and it creaked. The dogs were left behind in the cottage to make things easier. Jo noticed immediately that the house didn't feel right. It did not have the ease of a home with sunlight beaming through the windows. It had denseness in the air and a feeling that there were others there that could not be seen, eyes in the ether. Jo was on guard with a sense that anything could jump out from shadows, and she would be none the wiser before it came. It created a jumpiness within. Jo tried to release the feeling by taking in a deep breath, closing her eyes and gathering her senses and letting go of her fear. For that moment, the world disappeared.

She walked into the kitchen and placed the box on the table. Layce followed silently. She moved the chair away from the table and opened the box slowly. Things in this box were not only from Benin, but things she had learned along the way in life. She was a spiritual person. Perhaps that was what drew her to Clay from the beginning. He was also a spiritual man and had a deep rich life immersed in the roots of the Vodou religion. He grew up understanding ritual, celebration and rites of passage. He understood the spirit realm. Her spiritual box was filled with spiritual tools from his and the Native American culture. Her father was a half-breed and although they were young when he passed, he had lived long enough to share his Native American culture and his own spiritual ways with them. They were simple rituals of the sacred that were never really discussed but observed by her. Jo seemed to be the most connected to her father's spiritual life, although few words were ever spoken about it.

Her father's spirituality was more of a state of being and connectedness with nature and its need to change. Perhaps that was why she kept her spiritual life to herself. In a way, it was a way to keep her father to herself. It was a private relationship she could have alone, sharing it with no one.

"Jo, what's in there?" Layce whispered. Jo had never shared her spiritual life with her sister.

"Things Clay and Papa taught me."

Layce looked up at her when she mentioned their father. "Papa?"

Jo did not answer or look at her. Jo took out a pipe and placed Mishma into a wooden pipe, stuffed the pipe with the herb and lit it up with the lighter she pulled out from the box along with all the other ingredients. She sucked the flame into the pipe and drew in a breath with her eyes closed.

"You're smoking?" Layce whispered.

Jo felt her body going into a sort of trance. She was connecting already to something stronger. "The roots of the herbs run deep connecting us into the ground. The flame connects us to the elements of earth and the smoke

235

of them both connects us to the sky as it billows out and beyond."

Layce had never heard her sister talk this way before and it made her quiet. Jo handed her the pipe to partake. "It will protect us," she said to her sister and handed her the pipe. "It will help us ground and center our minds."

Layce took it in her hand and pulled in a breath causing the herb to burn a fire red. She expelled the smoke, and it floated up into the high ceiling. Jo took the pipe back in her hand and pulled out an ashtray to place the pipe on. Then she reached deeper down into the box and pulled out a ceramic bowl. Then a bag filled with a sage wand and lit it up. She handed Layce the bowl to hold and gave her no instructions. She grabbed the box and brought it into the living room and began her process. In each room, she moved the sage wand in the room. She placed an X in every window, door, mirror, and ceiling quietly saying a blessing, calling in her own energy and that of Layce's and sending all energy that does not belong in the house back to its source. She would then put the sage wand in the ceramic bowl that Layce held while she took out two bottles of liquid; blessed water and champagne.

Layce watched intently at her sister's intense focus and how she knew exactly what she was doing. She took the water and began to sprinkle the water in the four corners of each room.

"May this home be cleansed of any negative energy."

Then she took the champagne. "I apologize to this house and the land for all the tragedies that have happened here. I offer this to you in friendship," she said as she went from room to room downstairs, switching from smudging with the sage to the liquid offering. Not a spot was left that did not receive her cleansing,

Layce followed closely behind in a sort of student participation. They stood at the bottom of the stairs at the back of the house and looked up. It was time to go up, to where the real problem was. What they had done so far was mere practice.

Layce held the box under one arm and the ceramic bowl in the other. They climbed the steps slowly, knowing this would be the hardest part of the house to affect. As they reached the top of the staircase, the sage began to smoke more than it seemed to below to the point where the entire distance of the hallway was filled with smoke, so thick they could cut it, as if they were out on the water in the harbor morning fog.

It was unnatural. Sage or ectoplasm? The hall air felt thick, and Layce's hair began to fan out with electricity. They stopped a moment to acknowledge it. Then a chunk of Jo's hair was pulled straight up and quickly began to fold inside other strands on its own, as though a phantom child was braiding her hair.

"Jo," Layce cried out frightened. Jo was frightened too, but her sense of determination to take back her house from occupants who lived there longer than her, kept her moving.

The sound of a child's sinister laughter filled their ears, and the house echoed its eerie sounds. Her hair dropped back down. The smoke blocked the view down the hall, but down the hall they had to go.

"Continue on," Jo said sternly. She took the sage wand and began to do her blessing on the space, clearing the negative energy from the house and went into each room, even the bathrooms. Once she had smudged each room, she continued with the cleansing water and the friendship offering to the house. Each room was so dense with smoke that they could not see two feet in front of them, so they held close to one another. Wherever Jo went, Layce was right behind.

They went in and out of Layce's bathroom where the battle of the energies first appeared to Layce and then out they went, back down the hall. The hall was the most frightening place to be because it led to the room that they both knew was the object of their trouble. They needed to be in that room most of all but dreaded it the most. Neither said a word, but just moved forward.

They had gone in and out of the rooms and back into the hallway until they reached the cold room. The door was closed.

Jo stood in front of the door and said "open" to the door, but it did not open. She turned to Layce who held

Sufani Weisman-Garza

the sage bowl with the smoking wand, and Jo took the box from under her arm. From within the box, Jo placed the liquids back in and pulled out chalk. She began drawing on the door. Layce watched as she drew an ornate symbol on the door and the house began to creak and whine with disapproval. Walls and floorboards sounded as though they were twisting. She finished her drawing and placed the chalk back in the box and started singing: *"Paplaba Yey yey yey. Papblaba Yey yey yey,"* and other words that Layce didn't understand. She then picked up the chalk again and began to draw another symbol on the door. It looked like a grave with a cross on it and two coffins on either side standing up next to the cross. "The Gede will protect us," she told Layce. "Family of spirit guides, please be with us and help us cross these spirits over. Protect us from the negative energy. Shield us." She reached for the doorknob and twisted.

The latch opened and the door swung wide open like a mouth ready to devour them. The room was free of the fog that lay thick in the hallway and despite the opening of the door, no smoke entered from the hall, nor did it accept the sage smoke that had still been burning in the bowl. The room was different, pristine, transformed by time as though the house was showing them a time from the past. This was not the room that Jo decorated. It seemed a memory from a time long ago.

They walked into a movie of the house's history.

239

Toys lay scattered on the floor, a top, tricycle and disembodied doll torsos and heads. The room was eerily quiet and with great trepidation they entered, knowing it was some kind of trap.

They had to enter.

Jo took the sage from the bowl and the smoking sage wand had been snuffed out. She lit it again and as it began to smoke it was again snuffed out by some invisible force. The floorboards creaked as she began to walk around the room. The sound of an antique music box played in the distance with none in sight. She lit the sage again and this time it began to smoke, and she continued the practice of clearing the room and offering the sacred liquids. Layce kept close behind her sister, not trusting the room. They inched toward their target reluctantly.

"We have to go in the closet, Layce."

Layce shook her head. She was clearly afraid.

Jo understood her fear. Something in the room felt off – cunning.

"I'm going in. Something is in there. I have to end this." She took steps toward the closet and began to open it but it would not budge. She went under the sink and found a medal bar left by the last owner and quickly grabbed it and began to pry the door open. The sound that could only be described as a door tightening its grip and expelling pressure to remain closed began, making all the hardware in the closet twist and bend, creating creaks and pops of tension. The spirit of the girl resisted her prying fingers.

"Open your fucking door," Jo said, and she leaned into the tool to pry the door open. It fought her pressure, but she did not give up. Using all her strength she still could not open the door and she yelled out, "Lady in White … help me now." She stood back and the pops and creaks subsided – the door softly opened.

Jo dropped the bar in her hand, and it made a thud as it hit the ground. "Thank you," she said with a slick sweat on her forehead and brow. The room was filling up with smoke as it was in the hall and the room, although the windows that allowed in the sun, had become grey and dark. The opened closet door squealed, and she knew that she would need to go into the closet to the spot that had the loose board. It required her to walk in and pull the cord. Something in her was becoming more determined to overlook her fear. She walked in and pulled the chain to turn on the light. The same boxes that were left there laid in the same place.

"Layce," Jo said looking back at her, "put out the sage and put down the box."

Layce did as she was told.

Jo went directly to the loose wooden board, and she tried to use her nail to lift the board. She couldn't get it. "Layce, grab the bar." And she jammed her foot in front of the door as she exited the door just enough to get the bar,

241

making sure to not allow the door to shut leaving her sister in the closet alone. Jo took the bar and popped the wooden piece out. They both looked in; coming close to it, they found a hole six inches deep. At the bottom, there was a black velvet pouch. Jo and Layce looked at one another and Jo pushed her hand in the hole and brought out the pouch. She untied the bow that had held the pouch from unravelling and inside she found dentist tools, sharp utensils, tooth plyers. They were dirty and stained. As she looked closer and held it to the light, she dropped it, realizing that what she was seeing was dried blood.

She looked into the bag and saw pieces of hair, some attached with pieces of scalp. She vomited. "Oh," she said when she recovered and used her shirt to pull over her mouth.

"That was blood, Jo, wasn't it?" Layce asked.

Jo paused waiting for the nausea to pass. She took a deep breath and answered, "Yes." She took in a few more breaths and looked at the hole and noticed that beyond the spot in the wall, she saw that the hole looked like it went back even further. The wood exposed only slightly was not the same kind of wood, but a sort of flimsy plywood that did not match the wood of the walls in the closet. Those pieces were rich and healthy, beautifully solid and what was slightly exposed was the kind of wood used to cover up something. Jo reached for the bar again fully intending to find out what was there, and the bar forcefully

242

slid on the floor away from her hand. Layce slammed herself back against the wall getting out of the way of the bar that just moved on its own.

"Not today, bitch," Jo said getting up and walking over to the bar and grabbing it back into her hand and walking back to the wall to rip it out. She was done being bullied by some little ancient demon seed, or whatever the hell it was.

Forty-Two

With a restless anger, Jo walked back with the metal bar in her hand and applied it to the seam at floor level and began to pull. The panel began to tear away. A wind blew inside the enormous closet and the empty hangers on the poles began to swing and clank. The sound of a deep and hollow voice rang out in a humming, low and long tone:

"Nooooo!" The light in the closet began to flicker.

"Give me the box, quickly!" Jo yelled. Layce grabbed it and gave it to her. She pulled out a tiny hurricane style lamp and lit the wick. Just as the flame took, the light in the closet flickered out. Placing the lamp to the now exposed internal wall it became clear that it was a cemented looking wall. "What the hell is this?"

"Another room?" Layce asked and looked at her, stepping closer to the wall.

The cracking and creaking in the closet continued unnaturally as the house objected and the wind seemed to increase its intensity. A black mass began to form, and Layce ran to the door but it slammed shut. She began pounding on it and then turned around to see Jo facing it head on. She just waited there being nothing more she could do but wait to see what was going to happen. The mass was ceiling to floor and took shape into a six-foot shadow. She remembered the form from the first night she had been there. It was the man in the chair who she now knew was

244

the father, and from rumor, potential child murderer. Terror raced through her body and her heart raced faster.

Layce was silenced by fear.

"Oh my God," Jo let out, as she watched it take a more distinct form in front of her. The shadowy face looked at her and filled the room with its presence. Even the lamp was muffled by the shadowy existence of this Being and there was nowhere for Jo and Layce to go but to huddle together to provide some false sense of safety.

The shadowy figure said nothing. His loose form was enough to see a body, but not enough to provide a sense of the real man. He simply pointed his malformed and billowy finger at the exposed wall. The women looked at the wall. He was not attacking them; he was giving instruction. This did not feel like a threat from a serial killer, but instruction to break through the wall.

"But it's cement," Jo said out loud, trying to understand what she could possibly do.

Within seconds of her comment, the shadow figure formed a more distinct face and moved stealthily in front of her own and yelled out a wrathful instruction. "Go!" And he pointed his finger again to the wall more forcefully.

In sheer terror, Layce went to the wall of the closet and in a fit of provocation and her own fury, she began to kick the wall. As she did, pieces of cement and mortar started to crumble. There was a little beam of light that came through and as Jo saw this, she joined in kicking the wall down. What looked like a hard solid wall began crumbling, clearly having been weakened by its antiquity.

As the wall fell away, leaving a gap enough for them to crawl through, Jo bent down to take the plunge, only to be thrown up and back against the door of the closet. Layce ran to her to pull her away from the wall and the door to the closet began to open its heavy doors to thrust them out. The sound of childlike screams at a pitch that stung the ears was released. They covered their ears, but it scarcely helped. It was like the sounds of children screaming at the highest pitch they could; shrill cries that were frightening, and a warning to stay back, but they could not do that. They had come too far and gone through too much to stop now. The only way to reclaim the house was to uncover what had really happened in that home. What had happened to cause this battle of shadows? They needed to discover what was behind that wall.

Forty-Three

The sisters looked at one another and without words or hesitation they ran toward the hole in the wall and dove through its opening and into whatever lay in the retrograde. They were sweaty and dirty and found themselves in a pile of rubble and dust, as thick as a haunted abandoned mansion. They looked up from all fours and found that they were in a small, short hallway that had been sealed in.

"Jo. Look!" Layce pointed to what would be a left direction toward the back of the house. "How could this be here all this time and we didn't see it from outside?"

Jo did not answer; she simply came to her feet mesmerized and began to walk toward the dim light, Layce following suit. The hallway was dark but at the end of the hall was what appeared to be another door that was only slightly cracked open, enough to shed some stray light.

The activity had calmed. Perhaps it was too late for objections now because the room had been discovered. Whatever the girl did not want Jo to find lay on the other side of that door. Although she felt a sense of elation, she also felt a deep sadness come over her and a fear of what she was about to see. She knew that, whatever it was, it was not good and caused spirits to linger as a result.

The door at the end of the secret hall was a heavy thick wood, and the cobwebs created a gate almost thick enough to prevent them from entering. To open this door was to break an ancestral seal that had not been broken for what had probably been many generations. She slowly began to push the door open, disturbing the cobwebs, revealing a bright light entering the room. She saw small beams of light coming through cracks in what were boarded up windows directly in front of her. A six-drawer dresser was on the left of the door and covered with things an eight-year-old girl would love; musical jewel boxes, hats and barrettes strewn out across it, left in the exact place it had been on the last day of her life, cemented by dust. They walked in slowly looking around at the walls to the left and to the right hidden by the darkness, so much so that she could not see what else lay in the room. The lamp had remained in the outer closet, but Layce did not dare go back for it.

"Help me rip off some of this cover from the window," Jo instructed Layce. "I can't believe this is here," she said in a daze of shock.

As they both pulled off a piece of the board the room received only nominal light breaking through the dense brush in front of the window cleverly and purposely concealed but enough to see the room. They turned around to look closer at what had been covered in blackness.

"Oh my God," Jo let out, as she looked to the right of the window at the wall. More than half a dozen baby

248

dolls lay in their final resting place, hung in full dress and bonnets, period dress, on special hangers, on display. Others lay strewn on what looked like a small creative table where a child would normally cut construction paper in shapes, glue things or draw pictures.

This was not used for such innocent activities. These were no ordinary dolls on display. These dolls had decayed intact, on display in full dress, showing the bone and teeth where skin once had been. The missing children of the time lay hidden all these years in this room of death, by a demented ghost girl who had slain these children she had stolen from their homes, so long ago. The girl had always been the aggressor; the one causing fear.

The table lay with several more human dolls, some naked and some half-dressed. Teeth that were ripped out of their mouths lay on the table scattered with blood and dust. Dental utensils, no doubt stolen from her father, were used to pry out their baby teeth. These tortured children lay bloodied all over the table. Sharp dental tools used for scraping tartar off teeth were there surely used for some other design only the demented could think of. Once the full view and understanding of what she was seeing sank in, Layce let out a scream and terrible sobs.

"Oh my God," Jo said, and she began to cry. Overwhelmed with sadness, she understood what had happened. "She was a child-killer. The children that were missing! She tortured them … she killed them! Her parents found out what she had done." She paused, still looking around, touching nothing, putting it all together in her mind. She could not bear to take a closer look at the dozen or so children that lay murdered and ripped apart like they were indeed dolls to do with as she pleased. Children ranging in age from three months old to two, some with lips sewn shut with large spindle thread and eyelids sewn open – some of the skin was intact still, as though the children preserved some of their body, if only so someone could someday know what she had done to them. Skin above some of their lips had been sliced open revealing the gums—a piece of skin here and there, dried like beef jerky hanging off the bone, dried in place. Gums cut into, teeth exposed and ripped out, dried, ancient blood all over the tables and walls lay witness to the bloody carnage of this child killer. It was a scene of true horror. An evil so deeply seated within a person that no parent could take responsibility. An evil born into a child from some parasite serpent that hitched a ride and devoured the soul of whatever child was intended to be born was the only way to fathom a child who could do such a thing.

She was no ordinary eight-year-old and all signs had pointed to her from the beginning. The parents had surfaced only to protect and especially in moments when the girl had been present. They seemed to try to keep her at bay and lock her into the catacombs of her demented world behind the closet. The parent ghosts had tried.

Looking back now, it was so clear the parents had been warning Jo and her family. The innocent children were displayed in a way that was beyond eerie and comprehension. Hanging on the wall in full period dress from the 1800s, as they were when they had flesh, some facing out and one facing the wall; the baby that looked the youngest. Perhaps a glimmer of a conscience surfaced for a fleeting moment in her action against the most innocent of children; a three-month-old-looking baby, still in a baby bonnet. The Purdy girl was insane and clearly the parents had found out what she had done; found her secret slaughterhouse and dental room. What happened after that could only be a mystery now. But someone in the family knew because they went to great lengths to cover it up. Not even telling the parents of the dead children what happened to their babies. If they had, the children would have been removed.

But they lay in the exact place of their demise, a tomb untouched for over a hundred years in a room that once had a door but had become a chamber closed off with hopes of covering up the horror and sealing it off forever. Perhaps hoping it would disappear from the family history? They were almost successful. Did Nina Levensven know? She was strange, and it was her family, Mrs Purdy's side of the family, that took over the home. Surely, they were the ones who sealed off the room having been the next to live in it right after the murders. As she stood there

Sufani Weisman-Garza

with Layce, a mist began to accumulate and the angst filled them knowing what it meant, and the unpredictable nature of what would follow.

"Jo," Layce said, hitting her arm and pointing to the mist developing.

Jo stood ready for it and experience told her to look behind her to see what she could possibly be thrown into. But as the mist began to thicken the lady in white, and her husband in shadow, formed in the light – their images were transparent, but clearly seen. The Purdys were standing next to one another, as a couple, and as they took form only for a few seconds in the white mist, gentle smiles were on their faces and an expression that was grateful for what they had uncovered. They were not ghosts that were trying to hide anything; they were trying to free the spirits of the children and bring to light the truth of what had happened. They could be free now that the children were discovered. They could leave this mortal wound of their existence to better platitudes that only heaven held the secrets to. The energy in the room became calm and Jo did not fear for herself any longer. Layce clung to Jo's arm and they both took in the moment and somehow understood with no words that the worst was over, and now the ancient owners were moving on to a better place.

Jo knew with all her heart they were not murderers, as the reputation had been left to be assumed. It seemed perhaps the lesser of the evils for the family legacy. Better

Sufani Weisman-Garza

to have parents who went mad than to have a child serial killer in the family lineage. Perhaps that was the motivating decision that was made so long ago? Perhaps she would never know? As soon as Jo and Layce saw them appear and understood their effort to say thank you, the ghostly couple disappeared and seemed to move on. Jo felt their presence no longer in the house.

"Layce please go get the box and bring it in here," Jo said firmly.

"OK," Layce agreed and did as she was instructed. Layce returned with the box and Jo began to burn sage in the room, cleansing it, and as she did, she prayed for the children and told them they were now free, no longer captives to someone's madness. She handed Layce the blessed water and asked her to sprinkle it around the room and gently on the children in the room as she continued her prayer. She continued on with her ceremony to bless them and set them free, asking the house's forgiveness for so much violence within its walls.

"You're free now, children. Free from the terror you experienced. Go home now," she said in a tender voice to them. And in that moment the shadows that lay within their dead bodies began to shimmer a soft glow of light from their center and began to float out of their bodies. The white glow of their souls became fleshy beautiful faces. These young babies were like cherubs looking down upon them with smiles as they floated out of the room and into

253

a place greater than the dungeon of death, they had been subject to for so long. They were finally free.

After a few moments of silence, Layce asked, "What do we do now, Jo?"

Jo took in a deep breath and dared not to investigate the room further for fear of what she would see. Exhausted, she said, "We call the police."

Layce nodded and they left the hall, through the secret wall through the closet, out of the closet and headed into the cold room that no longer seemed cold. As they walked out of the room and into the hallway of the house, they heard the slam of a door. It was the door inside the secret chamber room. They both knew where it came from and that there was no draught to cause it. Neither said a word.

As they walked out into the hallway, they both went to the back staircase and looked at the wall that seemed to be the end of the house, now knowing that the secret room lay behind it. "Why did we not see this, Jo?"

Jo took a closer look at saw that where a hall had ended and a closet placed in, it created the effect that all the room left was enough for a closet because the kitchen vaulted. But it was an optical illusion. The blanket of hedgerows up against the house with Italian trees multiple layers deep, large evergreens, hydrangea bushes, ivy and other bushes that stayed full all year, coupled with a fountain and other landscaping gems that were so

254

whimsical that it led your eye away from the corner. You just assumed nothing more than shrubbery was there against the house. The trees covered the room and windows outside so thick that it was never seen from the outside or in. An amazing feat! Although other optical illusions were present in the architecture, like the walk-in closets. The oversized large ornate cabinet behind the staircase upstairs that was on an entire backwall also shielded a window close to the Cold Room window and now made sense as to why it was so different from the maids' cabinet. It was made at different times and for an entirely different reason. To block that area from view so no one could notice anything in that area and suspect and architectural missing space.

Jo had no more words to say, only enough to pick up the phone to call the police and her next call would be to Donovan; he was a comfort to her. She had just mourned the death of her own loved one, and now she would finally give rest to the families that surely wondered for hundreds of years what happened to the children, and family members who disappeared and were never found. It was a small town and should be easy to trace back missing children. Jo did not volunteer for this, but somehow was selected by the house ghosts to help families get closure to an ancient mystery. Perhaps it was her recent tragedy and sensitivity to the similar pain of losing someone she loved that made her the perfect Dick Tracy to uncover

Sufani Weisman-Garza

the mysteries of the house?

Now downstairs in the kitchen, Jo called the local police. Layce made tea trying to do something normal and then picked up her cell phone to call Ginni to get over there immediately.

"Hello?" Jo said. "I need to…report…" she took a deep breath "… dead bodies found in my home."

There was a long pause.

"You need to come and see this for yourself, officer," she said. "No. This case has been open for over a hundred years. They've decayed." There was another pause. "I'm the new owner of this house. 1377 Rikoppe Lane."

As she held the phone to her ear, she heard a thud. It came from the living room ceiling—the Cold Room. The hair on the back of her neck and on her arms stood up as she looked up forebodingly at the living room ceiling, not believing what she was seeing. Layce turned slowly to look with JoA black mass of ectoplasm was forming in the living room near the ceiling and a wind was kicking up out of nowhere and taking shape in the form of a funnel where the mass was. A strange electric noise began like something shorting out and sounds like locomotives passing through her living room got louder and louder. The ceiling began to shoot out light violently like pulses of a charge from some unseen source.

Dread filled every part of her being as the phone dropped from her fingers and she grabbed her ears.

Sufani Weisman-Garza

Something began shooting out of the ceiling fiercely and she could not believe her eyes. What looked like teeth were pouring from the ceiling out of thin air by the hundreds making the sounds of hard rain, as it hit the hardwood and carpets in the living room, ricocheting off tabletops of furniture. More teeth than bodies that could have had them pulled as if being materializing in a fit of anger. The distant sound of children crying could be heard, through the deafening noise. Layce and Jo stood frozen, speechless, exhausted, horrified!

"This isn't over yet!" Jo yelled, neither one of them taking their eyes off the ceiling. They both stood frozen in terror, hands over their ears, waiting for the police to arrive, and watching in horror as the mound of teeth piled up on the living room floor.

Sufani Weisman-Garza

1377 Rikoppe Lane

Get the Next Book In The Series

Purdy House| The Cold Room

Book 2

Sufani Weisman-Garza

Acknowledgements

I want to thank the McCall House in Ashland, Oregon, that inspired this entire journey of creating the Purdy House. When my husband and I stayed there several times, we fell in love with the feeling of the living history while being in it, the feeling of being back in time, reading the household ledgers and seeing pictures of the family and even hearing and reading some of their tragic history. We stayed in the room that became Jo's room, that was situated directly across from the 'Cold Room'. The floorplan of the McCall House was the basic foundation of the layout I used in my mind while creating the Purdy House on Rikoppe Lane. The house I chose visually is much larger and foreboding than the McCall house, and of course I embellished and changed many things, while always feeling I truly had been in the house I was writing about, because I had really been in it (minus additional rooms, décor and mysteries I added). I did have breakfast the next morning in the same dining room I recreated with a few guests, one of whom stayed in the room next to ours, and the guest spoke of being kept up by a ghost who was crying all night in her room. In my mind, it became the Crying Room, and this created more inspiration for a thrilling horror story I had just started writing. Although the setting in the book became Gig Harbor, in Washington State, which then borrowed some historical references there, like the name Purdy itself, the inside of the house in my story was all inspired by my stay at the McCall House. Thank you for such an inspiration. I will say that in an interesting way, I was called to the McCall house to write, as I was finishing another book that had been signed by an agent and did some writing there; I have a picture my husband took of me writing there. As I was finishing up the ending of that book. I was called to the McCall house, much in the way Jo was called to the Purdy House; for reasons that unravel over time.

I want to profoundly thank my editor, Carol Trow, for being a warm voice of reason, for fact checking me, for keeping my words meaningful and realistic. I tend to make up words or sometimes have completely different meanings for them until she set me straight. A good editor does more than check grammar, they check that what your characters are doing is what they would do in real life, they check that the facts make sense so it is believable, they question, instruct, are critical as needed and offer support and industry knowledge. I especially appreciate her support while leaving a publisher, re-editing and re-launching the first book. These two books deserved the best edits they could get, and she helped me achieve that. I also want to thank her for being there until we both said we were done. Her support was and is invaluable to me. Thank you so much for all your hours and efforts!

I want to thank my husband for the unending

260

support he gives me and knowing when to carve out undisturbed quiet time for me to write. From one artist to another, he understands me and what being an artist is (because he is one as well, with music) and so he understands the intensity of being in the middle of inspiration and how special that time is. I want to thank him for always understanding and honoring that space. I love him more than words could say!

I want to thank my sister Stacey, for always, and I mean always, being my biggest fan. She has always supported me in all my artistic endeavors and has read pretty much all my writings from the time I began. She has always encouraged me to live my dreams, to go for any inspired idea I've had, and showed up to any and every event I had, to be supportive. She bought my books when I would have given them to her because she wanted to support me. Someone like that is invaluable and I want her to know how much I truly love her (I do tell her all the time of course) and am so appreciative of all her support over the years. I love you, Sissy!

Thank you reader, for reading this book in any medium, and leaving me a review! I am so grateful for you.

More Books By Sufani

NON-FICTION

TRUE STORIES OF AN URBAN SHAMAN

RENEGADE OF LIGHT

GOOD SHOES IN THE VALLEY

FICTION

PURDY HOUSE| THE COLD ROOM

THE GREAT GATHERING OF GODS

SOUL

THE MANY REALITIES OF LOVE

Contact & Social Media

Email sufani@placeofblisssanctuary.com

Website: www.placeofblissacademy.com

Facebook: The Imperfect Author| SUFANI WEISMAN-GARZA | Facebook

Instagram: Published Author (@the_imperfect_author_sufaniwg) • Instagram photos and videos

Sufani Weisman-Garza

Made in the USA
Monee, IL
06 November 2023

45862929R00149